HARBINGERS 4.

The Girl

Alton Gansky

Bill Myers, Frank Peretti, and Angela Hunt,

Published by Amaris Media International.

Copyright © 2015 Alton Gansky

Cover Design: Angela Hunt

Photo © *elenaburn—Fotolia.com*

ISBN: 978-0692425602
ISBN: 0692425608

www.harbingersseries.com

HARBINGERS

A novella series by

Bill Myers, Frank Peretti, Angela Hunt, and Alton Gansky

In this fast-paced world with all its demands, the four of us wanted to try something new. Instead of the longer novel format, we wanted to write something equally as engaging but that could be read in one or two sittings— on the plane, waiting to pick up the kids from soccer, or as an evening's read.

We also wanted to play. As friends and seasoned novelists, we thought it would be fun to create a game we could participate in together. The rules were simple:

Rule 1
Each of us would write as if we were one of the characters in the series:

- Bill Myers would write as Brenda, the street-hustling tattoo artist who sees images of the future.
- Frank Peretti would write as the professor, the atheist ex-priest ruled by logic.
- Angela Hunt would write as Andi, the professor's brilliant-but-geeky assistant who sees inexplicable patterns.
- Alton Gansky would write as Tank, the naïve, big-hearted jock with a surprising connection to a healing power.

Rule 2

Instead of the four of us writing one novella together (we're friends but not crazy), we would write it like a TV series. There would be an overarching story line into which we'd plug our individual novellas, with each story written from our character's point of view.

Bill's first novella, *The Call*, sets the stage. It will be followed by Frank's, *The Haunted*, Angela's *The Sentinels*, and Alton's *The Girl*. And if we keep having fun, we'll begin a second round and so on until other demands pull us away or, as in TV, we get cancelled.

There you have it. We hope you'll find these as entertaining in the reading as we did in the writing.

Bill, Frank, Angie, and Al

Snow

January 1, 7:10 a.m.

"You're gonna love being a cop, Tank. Yes sir, you'll fit into the sheriff's department just fine."

I wanted to slap my forehead but I had too much respect for Uncle Bart. Instead, I kept my eyes directed out the passenger side window of the patrol car and took in the scenery.

"You don't even have to finish college, boy. Of course, that doesn't hurt nuthin', but I'm just sayin'."

That made me take my eyes off the snow-covered fields. "Momma wanted me to go to college, Uncle Bart. I gotta go. I *wanna* go. I like it."

"Hey, no problem, son. There's no rush. I could use you up here with me. I might just be a small town sheriff, but that doesn't make the work no less noble, does it?"

"No, sir. I admire what you do. I just don't know if I'm cut out to do it."

Uncle Bart—Sheriff Bard Christensen to everyone in Dicksonville, Oregon and the other small towns that make up the county—directed the car around a bend. I could feel the tires slip some and heard snow crunch beneath the treads. The tail end of the patrol car did a little fishtail.

Uncle Bart chuckled. "I love driving in this stuff. I wish we got more snow around here. Not enough to shovel you know, just enough to keep life interesting."

I released my grip on the door handle. To tell the truth, I had enough "interesting" stuff happen to last me a lifetime and I had a feeling more was coming.

"I didn't scare ya, did I, boy?"

"No, sir. I was just makin' sure the door didn't open. It might get dented or somethin'."

Uncle Bart smiled big. "Sure ya were, son. Sure ya were.

A few moments later, Uncle Bart turned serious. "I think that's him up there." He nodded to a man standing on the side of the road. He looked to be in his early seventies and wore a heavy wool coat over what I guessed was denim overalls. We pulled to the side and exited the car, then walked to the old guy. Yep, overalls.

"Sheriff." The man nodded. He had an accent. Maybe from the northeast. Maine?

"Mr. Weldon." Uncle Bart extended his hand.

"You can flush all the 'mister' stuff, Sheriff. Just Chuck. That's what everybody calls me. Chuck."

"Yes, sir." Uncle Bart smiled. "Chuck, this is my nephew, Bjorn Christensen but everyone calls him Tank."

"Ayuh, I can see why. You're a biggun', aren't you, son?" He looked puzzled. "Wait, ain't you the one who plays for the Huskies?"

I didn't know how to answer. Thankfully, he moved on.

"Not much of a college football man, myself, but the Sheriff here was telling everyone about you gettin' that football scholarship. He's real proud of you, he is. I hear that he'd lock up anybody that didn't want to listen." He followed the comment with a chuckle.

Uncle Bart came to my aid. "You called about something strange on your property, Mr. W—, um, Chuck."

"Ayuh, that I did. Could be real important so if you're done yappin' I'll show it to you."

"If *I'm* . . . yes, sir. Of course. Lead the way."

"Follow me." Chuck talked as he walked. "So, Tank, you gave up football to become a deputy?"

"No, sir. I'm just visiting." I was about a step and a half behind him. "Football is over for my team. We didn't have our best year."

"We watch the Rose Bowl together most years." Uncle Bart acted casual but I could tell he was scanning the ground. I knew why. When Mr. Weldon called he said there were some strange tracks Uncle Bart should see. "Probably just a three-legged rabbit," he had said. That was Uncle Bart's way. He made light of things. Everything.

"It ain't far, maybe another hundred yards or so. I was out this morning checking on my animals. I don't have many no more. Too old to take care of them. Too much arthritis. My feet ain't much good anymore. Sugar in the blood, don't ya know."

"Diabetes?" I said.

"Ayuh. I should've taken better care of myself, but I was always more concerned about the ranch. Ain't always been in the condition it is now. We used have a good number of cattle and other livestock . . ."

A sadness seemed to trip him mid-sentence.

"They give you pills for the diabetes?" It was none of my business but I couldn't help asking. Uncle Bart cut me a hard look. I shrugged.

"Stuff's expensive. The insulin is worse and all I got these days for income is my Social Security check, and there ain't much of that."

The sadness that seized Mr. Weldon turned on me. I felt like I should say something but couldn't put the right words together. Poor old guy had everything working against him: age, disease, and poverty.

"I got three things to show ya. Here's the first. I ain't gonna tell you anything about it. I'll let you jump to your own conclusions."

"Let me guess." Uncle Bart was smiling again. Maybe he was trying to lighten the moment. "Bigfoot came to visit."

"If he had he'd be lying dead in the snow. I'm old, but I can still shoot straight." He slowed. "Now watch yer step."

I had noticed that he stayed close to the tracks he had made when he walked to the road.

Mr. Weldon pointed. "As you can see, Sheriff, these ain't Bigfoot tracks. If anything, they're Littlefoot tracks. If you catch my drift."

I stayed close to Uncle Bart and looked at what Mr. Weldon was pointing at.

A chill rose inside me. It didn't come from the snow, or the stiff breeze coming off the nearby mountains. This cold started inside my bones and clawed its way to the surface. No heavy coat can keep out a chill that starts on the inside.

Uncle Bart swore.

"Yep. My sentiments exactly," Mr. Weldon said. "You see now why I called so early?"

I'm not one of those people who frightens easily, and Lord knows I've seen some pretty chilling stuff over the last few months. During football season, I face some pretty big guys. I'm big. Six-foot-three and a solid 275 but the guys I played against last season are bigger and meaner. There were several players on my University of Washington team that made me look small. Still, they don't frighten me. I like to think my faith has something to do with that, but this—

"Tell me what you see, Tank." Uncle Bart was testing me. For a moment I thought about giving a dumb answer, people are used to that from me, but this seemed too important. Besides, I didn't like the idea of trying to fool Uncle Bart. "Stop thinkin', boy, give me your first impressions."

"It's a footprint." I raised a hand. "I know, that part is obvious." It took me a moment to get the words to flow. "It's no animal. It's a human print. Small and—" The next part was difficult to say. "I can see toe prints."

"What does that mean to you, son?" Uncle Bart raised his gaze to me. Maybe it was my imagination but he looked almost as white as the snow on the ground.

"They're the footprints of a child. A child without shoes." I inhaled a lungful of cold air. "Uncle Bart. The kid is going to freeze his feet off."

He turned to Mr. Weldon. "Give me a sec, then I want to see what else you have to show me."

Mr. Weldon answered with a nod.

Uncle Bart raised the portable radio mike that hung from his shoulder to his lips, pressed the microphone key and reported what we had found. "I want everyone on this, Millie. I also want the helo up in the air. You know who to call for that."

I've met Millie several times. She's a nice fifty-something-year-old woman who has been the lead dispatcher for as long as I can remember. She always took holiday duty. I felt sorry for her at first, but now I was glad she was on the job.

"Chuck, how far did you follow the tracks?"

I could see a set of larger footprints running side by side with the kid's. The prints were not only larger but deeper, and I didn't have to be a detective to see the sole prints of the walker's boots. No doubt they belonged to Mr. Weldon.

"About a quarter mile, I'd say. Like I said, my feet ain't real good. I hate to admit it, but if I'd kept going I might be out there face down in the snow. Thought it the better part of valor to call you."

"Yes, sir. You did the right thing." Uncle Bart looked in the direction of the tracks. "Mr. Weldon—sorry, Chuck—I think me and Tank can move a little faster on our own. You've already been out in this stuff too long. If you don't mind, we'll go it alone."

"I had two other things to show you, but I appreciate it. Just follow the tracks. You'll come to a fence. You'll see what I saw. A little farther on you'll come to a barn. Take a moment there."

"We will, Chuck. We'll keep you posted."

Mr. Weldon started to go.

"Hang on a sec, Mr. Weldon." I stepped to him and placed a hand on his shoulder. "I'm sorry you're having a rough time. Maybe God will bless you for what you've done this morning."

He looked puzzled. "Um, okay, if you say so, Tank. I'm just doing what any man with a heart would do . . . Why is your hand so warm? It feels like you been holding a fresh out of the oven potato."

I shrugged. "Thank you again, Mr. Weldon." I released him and followed after Uncle Bart, praying all the way that we could find the child before frostbite had turned bare feet black.

Chapter 2

"This Ain't Right"

7:20 a.m.

We hadn't taken more than a dozen steps when the gray skies began shedding more snow. The wind picked up, too. I was wearing an extra police jacket, nylon on the outside and stuffed with whatever they put inside to keep a body warm. It kept the wind out, but couldn't protect my face. Snow and tiny bits of ice nibbled at my skin, and the cold wind was pushing through my jeans and trying to freeze the hair of my legs. I didn't focus on the discomfort much, not with some kid out here tromping through the snow with no shoes. Images fought for my attention and none of them were good. They all ended the same way: a dead child frozen in the snow. *Help us find the child, God. Please, please help us find the kid.*

Prayer is natural for me. I'm not from a religious family and I'm the only one of my friends who goes to church. Most just tolerate my beliefs; others poke fun at me. It makes no difference. Truth is truth and it remains that even if I'm the last one alive to believe it.

Uncle Bart, a man who could talk the ears off a statue, had gone silent and glum. I guess he had images flashing in his brain too.

"You're worried about the snow covering the tracks, aren't you Uncle Bart?"

He grunted. "It ain't making our job any easier. That's a fact." He didn't look up when he spoke. His eyes were glued to the impressions.

I walked on the left side of the small trail; Uncle Bart trudged along on the right. Like my uncle I had trouble tearing my eyes away. Still, from time to time, I scanned the white land in front of us hoping, praying to see a small figure still upright and moving. All I saw was a thickening blanket of white and split-rail fence sixty or so yards ahead. As we neared I could see the tracks continued on the other side.

We stopped at the fence. Uncle Bart squatted near the tracks and studied the ones closest to the fence. He rose and looked over the other side, careful not to touch anything. "This ain't right, Tank. Not by a long shot, it ain't."

"What ain't right?"

He started to say somethin' but held up. "You tell me."

"Uncle Bart, I don't think we should be wasting time testing my detective skills. I don't have any."

"Just look, boy. Look here." He pointed at the last two tracks closest to the fence. I did. "Now look at the ones on the other side. Do they look the same?"

I had no idea what he was getting at. All I could think of was the lost kid who was gonna need his feet amputated. Of course, I'd do what I could, but my gift is a little iffy. Sometimes it works, sometimes it doesn't.

"They look the same to me, Uncle Bart. What am I missing?"

"Should they look the same?" he pressed.

"I don't know, Uncle Bart, but I do know that if we don't find that kid—"

"I know what's at stake here, Bjorn. I don't need to be reminded. Just look."

He used my real name, something I hadn't heard him do since I was in kindergarten. So I looked. And I looked. The prints on the west side of the fence looked identical to those on our side.

Then I looked at the top rail of the fence. Two, maybe three inches of snow rested on the rail. The same amount on the rail to the north. The top rail to the south was different. Much of the snow had been knocked off. I could tell from Mr. Weldon's tracks that that was where he crawled over. The disturbed snow on the other side was proof of it.

"Do you see it?"

I nodded. "How is this possible?" I'm not the brightest crayon in the box but I'm not stupid, no matter what anyone else thinks. "If the kid climbed the fence, the snow on the rail would have been knocked off. Even if the snow continued, the amount on the rail would be less than that on the others."

"Right."

"So, maybe the kid just crawled through . . ." Dumb idea. Crawl through or climb over left the same problem. The snow on the rails would be very different than the snow on the rest of the fence. I moved closer and looked over the top rail. The tracks were unchanged. No sign of someone disrupting the snow by crawling through it, or jumping down from the fence. It was as if the kid had just walked through the fence, no, as if the kid had floated over the barrier.

"What's your take on this, Tank?"

I shook my head. All I could do was repeat Uncle Bart's words. "This ain't right." Then a second later I said, "We're not giving up are we?"

He narrowed his eyes but still managed to look disappointed. "Of course not, Tank. It's my job to gather information as I go. Who knows what will be important later?"

He scaled the fence and I followed by climbing the rails right in front of me. An easy job, but my foot was reminding me that I was still nursing a bad toe. A lineman showered his attention on me by pivoting his 300 pounds on that toe. I'm good now, but sometimes the toe likes to remind me it's there.

"I can't believe Weldon trudged all the way out here, not as old and sick as he is." Uncle Bart shook his head. "I have to admire the old coot."

"He's worried about the kid. He has a good heart."

"Yeah, I saw through that grumpy act pretty quick." Uncle Bart followed the tracks with his eyes. "There's the barn he mentioned. Let's pick up the pace, Tank. That toe let you jog?"

"I'm good to go."

We set off in a jog. Man, my foot hurt.

We reached the barn. It was an old building but someone had taken pretty good care of it. The wood was painted brown and the roof looked in good shape, at least it didn't bow any. The blanket of snow concealed the roofing material beneath—

What?

I blinked a few times. Then turned to face Uncle Bart but he was rounding the barn. He reappeared a few moments later. "The tracks continue on the other side. You know why that's impossible, right?"

I didn't answer; I backed away from the building.

"What's wrong, Tank?"

I pointed to the top, to the snow, to the footprints walking up the slope of the roof.

Uncle Bart followed my example and stepped back from the barn. He stared at the tracks on the roof then looked at me. At first he said nothing. He returned his gaze to the roof, then the tracks on the ground. More silence, then a string of curses lit up the air. I didn't interrupt.

I no longer felt cold. I no longer noticed the wind or my almost healed broken toe. I was numb, not from the freezing air but from being forced to face the impossible—again.

"This is a joke, Tank. It has to be some kinda sick joke. And when I find out who's behind it, I'm gonna kick his butt from here to Mexico and back . . ." He went on like that for a couple of minutes. He got hotter and his language got worse. I used the time to restart my brain.

The fence with the undisturbed snow was too much to take in, but this, well, this almost shut me down. From the looks of things, the kid we were tracking flew over a fence and, apparently, onto a roof. Maybe Uncle Bart was right, this was all a gag, a joke played on the sheriff. If so, then I could understand Uncle Bart's reaction. Of course, I wouldn't help him kick the perpetrator's butt up and down the west coast, but I probably wouldn't stop him from doing so. The way I felt at the moment, I'd be willing to sell popcorn at the event.

"Now we know why Mr. Weldon told us to take a few moments here." My voice sounded strange to me. I hoped I sounded normal to Uncle Bart. "I'm gonna check out the other side of the barn." I had to assume that there was still a kid missing. If Uncle Bart was wrong and we turned back, then we could end up finding someone's kid dead and alone. Before I rounded the corner, I saw Uncle Bart remove his smartphone and start taking pictures.

On the other side of the roof were the same kind of tracks descending the slope. They went right to the eave, then picked up on the ground as if the hiker had twenty-foot long legs with tiny childlike feet. The image would have been funny if I wasn't standing in ever-increasing snow with a missing kid on my mind.

I looked at were the tracks on the ground picked up. I had learned a couple things from Uncle Bart's insistence that I study the fence. This time I didn't need his encouragement. I did my best to look for clues but the only thing I saw was the same set of tracks as we had been following. The stride was the same. The impressions the same. No sign that someone jumped from the roof. If this was a gag, then the guy pulling the joke was good. Really, really good.

I heard an electronic squawk, then a voice. Uncle Bart was on the radio. He rounded the barn, then looked up beyond the roof to the slate gray skies. First came a thumping sound like rhythmic thunder, then I spotted the Sheriff's helicopter.

"We'll have answers soon." Uncle Bart watched the craft sail overhead directly over the tracks.

"Did he see anything on the way in?"

Uncle Bart shook his head. "They disappear two miles up the trail. Just disappear in the middle of a snow-covered field. I have him looking for other tracks. Didn't make much sense to the pilot, but I told him nuthin' about this makes sense.

He was right about that.

Chapter 3

Found and Lost

7:52 a.m.

The warmth of the patrol car felt good even though I worked up some internal heat jogging back with Uncle Bart. The helicopter pilot had told us the tracks we were following ended two miles farther on from the barn. That was too far to trudge in the snow. Driving made more sense. Under Uncle Bart's order, the copter kept searching. Maybe the kid transported or whatever to a place nearby. I would have thought that was a stupid idea if I hadn't seen what I had seen.

"You okay, Tank?" My uncle steered the patrol car down the slick road, moving faster than he should. Earlier he said he loved driving in these conditions. He didn't look like he was having as much fun now.

"I'm worried about the kid." I didn't look at him. I needed to keep myself together for Uncle Bart—for the kid in the snow.

"You always did have a big heart. Maybe too big."

"You're not worried?"

He pushed his lips in and out a couple of times. "Yeah. I'm worried."

I believed him. I could hear it in his voice. Truth was, he had a pretty big heart himself, especially when it came to children. He and Auntie June never had kids. It wasn't talked about in the family but it was assumed that they were just one of the couples who couldn't have kids. All that love he would have had for a son or daughter got lavished on other people's children and me. Lord help anyone who hurt a child in Uncle Bart's presence.

He let off the gas and let the car slow under its own weight. A couple of moments later he tapped the brakes. Anyone who hit their brakes on an icy road like this was looking for an expensive tow home. As the car slowed he flipped on the light bar. Red and blue splashes of light danced on the snow and the trees that lined the south side of the road. He pulled onto the shoulder facing oncoming traffic—if there had been any—and let the car slide to a gentle stop.

"Let's go."

He was out of the car before I could unbuckle my seatbelt.

I had to jog a few steps to catch up to him. He plunged into a small stand of trees, the one the copter pilot told us about. He slowed, glanced around. "I'm going south, you go north. Maybe the kid ducked in here to get out of the snow."

The logical thing for me to say was, "But the kid's tracks stop in the middle of the field. The pilot told us so." I didn't say that. Why would I? I had seen the fence. I had seen the barn. For all I know, the kid flew to the moon. Once you cross over into the world of the impossible, you learn that anything can happen. I've been in a house that came and went as it saw fit, seen thousands of eyeless dead fish wash up on shore in

18

Florida, and equally eyeless birds fall from the sky. I've seen and been attacked by evil beings in a place that was supposed to be a school for gifted kids. These days I can believe the impossible without raising a sweat.

"Got it." I looked at the ground. I searched behind trees. I peered under bushes. The good news: I didn't find a body. The bad news: I didn't find anything. The stand of trees was not large, just the left overs from when some farmer cleared an area for his crops. That probably happened decades ago. Some farmers and ranchers left trees up for a wind block.

I wove my way through the trees, ignoring the snow bombs they dropped on me, and saw nothing. The whole time I prayed for help, but I couldn't seem to get prayers above the tops of the trees. Once I reached the edge of the tree stand, I turned and worked my way back, taking a different path. When I got to where I started, I found Uncle Bart waiting for me. His expression told me he found no more than I had.

"I wanna take a look at those tracks in the field. I don't know that it'll do any good, but I don't want to overlook anything."

There was little more that he could do. The helicopter was still searching and every deputy in the region was driving the roads and lanes. I even heard Uncle Bart ask Millie to call up the volunteer search-and-rescue team. They would soon be searching using horses, dogs, and off-road vehicles.

We slogged through the snow, leaving a set of our own tracks behind us. Ours and the kid's were the only tracks visible. The kid's steps just ended in the middle of the field. He had disappeared.

"It's like the kid just evaporated into thin air." Uncle Bart was sounding discouraged and angry. "I see it with my own eyes and I still don't believe it. This is impossible. I'm starting to question my sanity."

Before I could offer any encouraging words his radio crackled to life. It was Millie from the station house.

"Sheriff, you need to return to town."

He keyed the mic. "I'm not coming back until I have found this kid."

"That's just it, Sheriff. We found her. She's in town. Standing in the middle of Main Street."

"How do you know it's the same kid?"

"Well, she's a kid and she's barefoot."

"I'm on my way. Get an ambulance. She's gonna need medical care."

"We can't get close to her, Sheriff. She goes nuts if anyone approaches."

Uncle Bart paused, then, "You try, Millie. Maybe she'll respond to a woman."

"I thought of that, Sheriff. She doesn't like me or any other woman any more than she does men."

"I'm on my way. Keep people away from her. I'll come up with a plan."

We sprinted, as much as the snow would allow, back to the car. Uncle Bart added a siren to the lights and had us motoring down the road in moments.

"She's alive," I said. "Thank God, she's alive."

"I got a strange feeling about this, Tank. I don't know why."

I had a guess, but I kept it to myself.

The drive back didn't take long but even with traffic pulling over for us, it seemed to take a day and half. Time is funny that way. We pulled into Dicksonville and onto Main Street just a few blocks past the Sheriff's station.

The first thing I noticed was a patrol car pulled across the centerline of the street in a one-car roadblock. Made sense. If the girl was in the middle of the street then someone had to stop traffic. I assume another deputy had done the same farther down the road.

The presence of the deputies was no surprise. Uncle Bart had ordered them to return to town. He wanted eyes on the girl. Slowly, Uncle Bart pulled around the parked patrol car and crept forward. People in the street stepped aside for him.

A short distance away, I saw a circle of people surrounding a child. My heart broke. Being surrounded had to be terrifying. "No wonder she's upset. She's like a trapped animal."

"I was thinkin' the same thing, Tank."

We exited the patrol car. A uniformed deputy approached. "Hey Sheriff."

"Hey, Wad. Fill me in."

Deputy Waddle—everybody called him Wad which I don't think he liked but put up with—was tall, wiry, and had an inflated Barney Fife ego. He wasn't the nicest guy I've met. Uncle Bart once told me that Wad was a pimple on most people's butts. I've had trouble shaking that image.

"Hey, Tank. How's college life—"

Uncle Bart cut him off. "Focus, Wad."

"Yes, sir. I was first back from the field. Someone reported a child in the street. When I arrived I tried to move her to the sidewalk. Didn't work out so good."

"What do you mean you tried to move her?"

"You know, Sheriff. I tried to pick her up and carry her to the side. She went ape on me. I had to back off."

From the look on Uncle Bart's face I could tell he had a few words for Deputy Wad but he swallowed them whole. "Let's get the crowd back. They're making me nervous, and if they make me nervous they gotta be terrifying the girl. Move 'em back, Wad. Let's give the kid a little room to breathe.

I followed Uncle Bart, but stayed well back of the kid. She didn't need a mountain like me towering over her. Once the crowd cleared I could see the little girl. She looked to be about ten, had blonde hair that parted down the middle and hung to her shoulders. Her hair was wet, which made sense since she had been in the snow. She wore a white, short-sleeved blouse, the kind with frill on the sleeves. I'm sure women have some name for it, but I don't know what it is. She also wore jeans. They were soaked below the knees.

It took a moment for me to muster the courage to look at her feet. A glance told me she wore no shoes, but I needed to look closer. I expected to find red skin on its way to frostbite black. I didn't see that, but then I was several yards away. I knew she had been in the cold long enough to need medical care. A short distance down the street sat the ambulance. The EMTs were near the vehicle, waiting to be called in.

The little girl watched as gawkers backed away. She made no attempt to flee. Instead, she stood on the blacktop as if she had grown roots. She seemed free from pain and the effects of the cold wind swirling down the street. She did, however, looked concerned, eyeing everyone in her line of sight. Uncle Bart smiled at her. He was a man with a friendly face and nonthreatening manner. If anyone could gain her trust, he could.

Or so I thought.

He held out both hands, showing that he held nothing that could hurt her. He took a step forward and for a moment I thought she would scream. Uncle Bart stopped. "Okay, okay, little one." He took a step back then dropped to one knee. "Nobody is gonna hurt you. I'm your friend." He pointed at his badge. "See, I'm a policeman. Children can trust policemen." He spread his arms like a parent calling for a hug. The kid didn't move.

She stayed put, her gazed fixed on him. She raised one arm across her chest. At first I thought she was mimicking Uncle Bart's movement when he pointed at his badge, then I noticed she was holding something. I couldn't make it out. It reminded me of a scroll. A scroll of brown paper.

"Maybe I should go around behind her." It was Deputy Wad. He was moving in Uncle Bart's direction.

Uncle Bart smiled at the little girl, held up one finger and turned to Wad. He spoke softly but his tone was as sharp as a razor blade. "I told you to get back."

Wad retreated, looking like a scolded dog.

Uncle Bart turned back to the girl. "My name is Mr. Christensen. What's your name?"

Nothing.

"I'm the sheriff here, sweetie. That means it's my job to take care of people. Especially little girls like you."

No response.

"Do you know where you're mommy and daddy are?"

Nothing doing. I was beginning to think that she might be one of those special kids—special needs kids, they call them. That thought broke my heart all the more. This little girl needed a friend.

It was a standoff in the streets of Dicksonville with the sheriff on one end of the street and a ten-year-old girl on the other. The girl was winning.

A motion caught my attention. While we were watching the drama in the street unfold, Deputy Wad had worked around the crowd and pressed through the citizens until he was behind the youngster. His intention was clear: he was gonna rush the girl.

Uncle Bart saw him about the same time I did. His eyes went wide for a moment, then his brow dropped like a guillotine.

"Wad, I told you—"

Wad charged for all he was worth, which isn't much, but it would have been enough to hurt the girl had he caught her. He didn't.

She was gone.

Then she was back, standing twenty feet in front of me. She glanced back at Wad, who had slipped on the ice and executed a perfect, five-star face plant on the snow-covered pavement. I'm ashamed to admit this, but it was a good thing to see.

The girl turned to face me. She looked into my eyes and something hot, scorching, flooded my soul. I felt weak, confused, and a bit dizzy, the kind of dizzy I get when I crack helmets on the field. It kinda made my bones go soft.

I cocked my head to the side. She did the same.

Then she was in my arms.

I don't know how. Don't ask. I didn't see it coming. Didn't see it happen. One moment we were staring at each other; the next she was in my arms, her tiny arms wrapped around my neck.

It was the best hug I ever had.

"Um, hi little girl."

She remained silent.

"People call me Tank. What should I call you?"

She tightened her grip around my neck. I got the feeling she wasn't afraid of me, she was just giving me another hug. She buried her face in my neck. I knew then and there, I'd move mountains for her.

"That's all right. You can tell me when you're good and ready. Until then I'll call you . . . what?" My mind jumped back to our conversation with Mr. Weldon when Uncle Bart was joking about Bigfoot. He said something like, "More like Littlefoot." I chuckled. "How 'bout I just call you Littlefoot because of all the tracks you left in the snow?"

Another hug. I took that to be a *yes*.

The next bit of business scared me the most. "I need to look at your feet. I won't hurt you. I promise."

I did my best to examine her feet, best I could while holding her to my chest. I saw enough.

Perfect.

No injuries. No cuts. No damage from the snow. Her feet looked like they had never touched anything more harsh than a plush carpet. There was great joy in that.

Uncle Bart approached but kept some distance between so as not to spook the girl. "I'm not sure what I just saw."

"Me neither." I gave the girl a little squeeze. "This is my Uncle Bart. He's a real good guy. I trust him and I hope you'll trust him too."

She turned her head so she could see him.

Uncle Bart removed his uniform hat and bowed, bending deep at the waist like he was bowing to the queen.

"Uncle Bart, this is Littlefoot. At least for now."

"A pleasure to meet you, Your Highness."

Then a real miracle happened.

Littlefoot smiled. It might be my imagination, but when she did the sun came out and a spring breeze rolled down the street.

I Almost Failed French

8:45 a.m.

We returned to the Sheriff's substation, me walking with the little girl in my arms, and Uncle Bart driving. It wasn't a long walk and I found it easy to carry her. After the heavy weight of worry I had been living with since I first saw her bare footprints in the snow, she seemed light as a feather. She hung on me for all she was worth and kept her face buried in my neck. I could feel the rolled-up paper rub against my skin. I wondered about it, but it was a wondering that could wait.

The paramedics followed Uncle Bart to the station. I know it would have made more sense to examine Littlefoot for injuries in the ambulance but she made it clear—real clear—she wanted nothing to do with it. I suggested the station because it would be warmer there and out of view of the rubberneckers who seemed to come from nowhere and everywhere.

Millie was waiting for us, holding down her spot at the dispatch radio.

The station was larger than most expected for such a small town. There were four jail cells in the back. Uncle Bart told me people don't stay there long. They were just holding cells. The front office had several desks, a large one near the middle of the room where a deputy was assigned to deal with walk-ins. Uncle Bart had a private office in the back. There was a small kitchen tucked away out of sight, and a small lunchroom. Of course, there were a couple of bathrooms. The walls were covered with dark-wood paneling, something my uncle called, "Early 70s crap."

Deputy Wad showed up a few moments after we entered the station. He had a decent size scrape on his right cheek and his nose looked a tad swollen. One paramedic, a woman named Beth, took a look at him, examining his cheekbone to see if he busted it up. I know that had to hurt but he gave no sign of it. If I was into gambling, I put money on the fact that if the paramedic had been a guy, Wad would have been swearing like nobody's business. In football, I've taken a few shots to the head and can't say I liked it.

The second paramedic, a middle-aged man Uncle Bart called Jim, examined Littlefoot, or least *tried* to examine her. She pulled away every time he tried to touch her. The female paramedic gave it a try, which I think should have been the way to start the whole thing, but had the same bad luck.

"Let's try this," I said. Littlefoot was sitting on my lap. I gave her a little hug and a big smile. She blinked a few times and I felt her body relax some. As gently as I could I took hold of her right ankle and lifted her foot. The paramedics stared at it, shining a beam from a small flashlight on the skin. We did the same thing with her left foot.

"No cuts and no signs of frostbite." Jim shook his head. "Skin is not even red. You sure she's been hiking through the snow?"

"Several miles," Uncle Bart said. "Tank and I followed the trail for over a mile before . . . before returning to the car to check the roads."

I wouldn't have mentioned the strange way the tracks disappeared myself.

"Her feet are fine," Jim said. "I need to take her temperature, Tank. Any ideas how I do that?"

I had an idea. "Take mine first."

Jim nodded as if he thought it was a good idea. He removed one of those new thermometers they rub on your forehead. I was glad to see that. I gave Littlefoot's shoulder a little squeezed and leaned forward. Jim ran the device over my skin then showed the readout to the girl. "A little low, Tank, but considering you've been tromping through the snow, I'd expect your skin to be a little cool."

He handed the device to me and looked at Littlefoot. She studied it for a moment, looked at my forehead, cocked her head again, then seemed to come to some understanding. She tilted her head back and let me run the digital thermometer across her forehead. I handed it back to Jim.

"Normal. Interesting. It's right on the money." He looked puzzled. "Well, that's good." He removed a small blood pressure tester, the kind the fits on a person's wrist. I held out my arm. He looked at my wrist. "Um, I hope this fits."

It did, but not by much. It ran its test giving my blood pressure and pulse rate. He handed it to me and Littlefoot immediately held out her free hand but kept the one with the scroll close to her chest. That kinda trust can bring a tear to a man's eye.

Jim looked at the message while Beth jotted down the info. "Normal." He grinned and tried to pat Littlefoot on the knee, but she pulled away. He jerked his hand back, then sighed. He rose, picked up his medical kit, and turned to Uncle Bart. "That's about all I can do, Sheriff. She's responsive, I see no injuries—"

"Why doesn't she talk?" Uncle Bart asked. The question carried unspoken companions with it.

"I can't say, Sheriff. She could have a learning disability, or she might be mute. She seems to track with our voices and other sounds, so I doubt she's deaf. She looks well fed, not fat, but not starved. Skin tone is good. I don't have answers. She needs to be tested in a hospital by doctors."

"I assume you'll be calling child protective services," Beth said.

"Of course. Somebody somewhere is probably worried sick about her."

Millie broke her silence. "That's the thing, Sheriff. No one has reported a missing child."

"It's still early, maybe her parents are sleeping off last night's party."

"If that's the case CPS is going to raise a real stink." Uncle Bart thanked the paramedics.

"Glad to help." Jim glanced at Littlefoot again. "I hope you get it all straightened out. She's a cutie. Gotta love those blue eyes. I'm afraid though, that someone may have abused the tyke. I don't like saying that."

"It occurred to me," Uncle Bart said. Unfortunately, it had occurred to me too.

The paramedics left the office, closing the door behind them.

I was thankful for their help—blue eyes? I looked into the face of the angel sitting on my lap. She looked back at me through her big brown eyes.

Under Uncle Bart's order, Millie called Child Protective Services. It was New Year's Day so the process was moving slowly. I set Littlefoot in my seat and pulled up another straight-backed chair so I could face her. Her blond hair, big brown eyes, and round face made her appear angelic. I don't know if I will ever have kids. I like the idea, but who knows what the future holds. If I do, I hope God will give me a little girl like the one staring at me.

"My name is Tank," I said and pointed to myself. Maybe I could get her to open up. I doubted she had a learning disability, although I'm certainly not qualified to say that. Call it a feeling if you want.

I repeated myself and tapped my chest: "Tank." I pointed at my Uncle: "Uncle Bart." I probably should have called him Sheriff Christensen, but that seemed like too much of a mouthful. Then I pointed at her. Nothing.

I tried again and then another time. Nothing. No name. No words. Still, I felt certain she understood.

Uncle Bart inched closer. "What about the paper, Tank? You think you could get that from her?"

"I dunno. It seems real important to her, Uncle Bart."

"I noticed. She hangs on to that thing like your Aunt June hangs onto a dollar."

Wad cleared his throat. "You want me to just grab it from her, Sheriff? It would only take a moment."

Uncle Bart turned. "Deputy Waddle, I assume that comment came because of the injury to your head. If I were you, I wouldn't argue with me about that."

"Yes, sir." Wad didn't sound all that genuine.

I gazed at the paper, then motioned to it. To my surprise, she held it out to me. Uncle Bart stepped forward and tried to take it, and she pulled it back just as quick. When he backed away, she held it out again.

I took it. "Thank you, little one."

The scroll was a single piece of brownish paper rolled into a tight tube. I opened it slowly and with great care. No telling what she would do if I tore the thing. The page was about the size of a legal pad. There were letters, or pictures, or picture-letters, I didn't know what to call them.

"Doesn't look like anything I've ever seen." Uncle Bart was looking over my shoulder. Wad came close too. "What about you, Tank? Seen anything like it in those college classes you take?"

"No, sir, but then again I almost failed French. I have enough trouble with English, let alone a foreign language." I tapped the odd paper. "Especially something as weird as this."

Wad weighed in. "Maybe it's an alien language."

"You mean like from Canada." Uncle Bart was good with sarcasm.

"Of course not, Sheriff. That's ridiculous. I mean like from outer space. You know, like a UFO or something."

"Yeah, that makes much more sense than an alien from Canada." If Uncle Bart's tone wasn't so dark, I'd think he was having fun with Deputy Wad.

"I bet Tank agrees with me, don't ya?"

I glanced at Wad and shrugged. "After this last year, I've stopped ruling things out."

Uncle Bart straightened. "What's that supposed to mean?"

"Long story, sir." I looked back at the girl and smiled. She didn't respond. I looked back at the weird paper with the odd markings. "I know who might be able to help. Several someones."

My cellphone chimed. A text:

On our way. Will be there in the morning.

It was from Andi. The sight of her name made my heart trip. I replied with a text of my own: *How did you know?*

Before I could ask, another text appeared on my smart phone.

We're all coming. Daniel, too.

I assumed by *all* she meant Dr. McKinney, too.

Another chime. *I will explain when we get there.*

I was already pretty freaked out by the day's events, but knowing my friends were coming without a clue as to why I needed them kinda shook me. Still, I couldn't wait to see Andi—and the others.

Uncle Bart was staring at me. "Judging by that befuddled look on your face I assume that the message was unexpected."

"Yeah. Help is on the way, Uncle Bart."

Wad asked, "What kinda help? The feds?"

"I don't know any feds." I put my phone away. "These guys are better than the feds."

Chapter 5

A Burger and Shake

10:30 a.m.

"A priest?" Uncle Bart sounded stunned. "What's a good Lutheran boy like you doin' hanging with a priest?"

"Well, he used to be a priest," I explained. I reached for Littlefoot's hand. She didn't hesitate to take it. That made me feel good and so did the warmth of her touch. For the life of me I couldn't figure out how she could have been walking through the snow and wind without feeling like a bag of ice water. "He gave that up."

"He left the priesthood?"

I followed Uncle Bart into the small break room. "Yep. He gave up on God. Decided to be an atheist. He thinks that's what smart people do." I lifted Littlefoot into one of the chairs and pushed it close to the battered table. I guess the table is older than half the town.

"You know me, Tank, I ain't much on church going, but I don't think I've turned my back on God. I may not be as religious as you, boy, but I still got my beliefs."

I started to tell him that faith and religion weren't the same thing, but it didn't seem the time to have that conversation.

"Who are these other people?" Uncle Bart took a chair at the end of the table. No matter what table he sat at, he sat at the head. I suppose it was a control issue. No one complained, but then it would have done no good to do so. Uncle Bart did whatever Uncle Bart wanted to do.

"I'll introduce you to them when they get here. They're good people, but they're a little—different."

"Different? How?"

The best I could do was shrug. "I'm not sure I can explain it. I'm not sure I understand it all. I trust them. I've had to."

"Now, boy, you're gonna have to explain that. There's gotta be a story behind that statement."

A story? As old man Weldon would have said, "Ayuh." Except I didn't say it out loud. A story. How could I tell him about the unusual people I'm hangin' out with these days. A professor, a tattoo artist, a kid who sees strange people, and a young lady with a mind that chews information like a computer.

"Uncle Bart, have you ever seen anything you couldn't explain?"

He leaned back. "Well this thing with the girl qualifies, but I've seen a thing or two, yes."

"Do you tell people about it?"

"Not really."

I nodded. "It's not that I don't want to tell you, but I just don't know how, not in a way that you'd believe. Maybe the others can do a better job than me."

I heard the door to the station open and close. The sound of it came with the smell of cooked meat. It was a tad early for lunch, but we were up early and hadn't eaten. Add to that the fact that we hiked a long ways in the snow and endured some real emotional strain, so we were beyond hungry. We also needed to make sure Littlefoot had some food. She had to be hungrier than us. We also wanted to be able to tell CPS that we had done right by the little girl.

I smiled at her. She didn't smile back, but she did blink those lovely eyes— Hazel? Weren't they brown? I remembered the paramedic calling her eyes blue.

"Chow is here, guys." Wad walked into the break room struggling to carry several bags of food and a tray of drinks. "Burgers and shakes."

My stomach did a couple of flips of joy.

"Thanks," Uncle Bart said and reached for one of the drinks.

Wad sat at the foot of the table. Littlefoot eyed him for a moment, then looked at the bags of food. I removed a small cheeseburger, unwrapped it, setting the wrapper on the table like a napkin, and then set the burger on top of that. She looked at the burger as if she expected it to get up and move. I took a chocolate shake and inserted a straw, then placed that near the cheeseburger. I felt a bit of guilt about giving her this kind of food. I probably should have asked for something healthy. That's me. I have tons of great ideas; I just have them about a half-hour after they're needed. Besides, what kid doesn't like a burger and a shake?

I took a sip of my shake, placing the business end of the straw in my mouth and watching Littlefoot. It's hard to say why, but I had a feeling that all of this was confusing her. I took another sip, smiled, and said, "Yum." I pointed at her shake. She pulled it close, lifted it from the table, put the straw in her mouth and waited. Of course, nothing happened.

"You gotta suck, kiddo." I showed her again, exaggerating the way to use the thing. She got it on the second go around. I watched the chocolate ice cream rise in the clear straw.

She set the cup down and frowned, then she smacked her lips and stuck out her tongue a few times like a dog trying to get peanut butter off the roof of its mouth.

"No doubt about it," Wad said, "the kid is missing a few marbles."

I may play football, but I don't believe in violence. Not usually, anyway. Wad was giving me a reason to change my point of view.

Uncle Bart was staring at him. "I need a favor, Deputy."

"Sure, Sheriff, what can I do for you?"

"You can keep your opinions to yourself. Eat your burger, then get back on patrol."

"All I'm saying is . . ."

Uncle Bart's expression made Wad trail off.

"I think I'll go eat with Millie." Wad rose from his chair and left.

Uncle Bart didn't try to stop him. I saw no reason to insist he stay.

Littlefoot repeated her actions: sip, frown, followed by tongue gymnastics. I don't think it tasted bad to her. It was as if she had never seen a milkshake or burger. She tried the sandwich, first licking the bun, then the edge of the meat patty.

It broke my heart. Littlefoot was as innocent as any child I had ever seen. Where had she been living that she didn't know what a burger and milkshake was? A vision of the child locked in a closet for years invaded my brain. A stew of emotion boiled in me. I was glad she was safe; I was pleased she was unharmed; my heart ached at her simplicity and confusion; and I was furious that anyone would let a child grow up this way.

I think Uncle Bart was reading my expression or something because he spoke in a tone softer than I was used to hearing from him. "You've been a big help, Tank."

"I ain't done much. Just showed the kid a little kindness."

"Don't sell yourself short, boy. The world can use a little more kindness, especially the kind you've got. That little girl took to you when she'd have nuthin' to do with anyone else. She sees you as a friend."

"Well, I'm not wearing all the police gear you are. I'm just a big teddy bear."

Uncle Bart laughed. "Is that what they call you on the football field?"

I looked away. I didn't want to talk about football. Littlefoot watched me bite into the burger. Man, the cafeteria made a good cheeseburger. She cocked her head, then picked up the food and nibbled a bit of the bread. She set it down while she chewed as if examining some strange object. She picked it up it again and this time took a bigger bite. She was getting the hang of it.

"What's going to happen to her, Uncle Bart?"

"You can't keep her, Tank. She's not a puppy."

"I know that. I'm just worried about her. She's so innocent."

"Social services will be here soon. They'll get her set up all nice and comfy. Soft bed, warm covers, toys, whatever she needs." He paused. "You think she'll go along with them easily? I hate to think of them picking her up and putting her in the back of the car. I've seen it before— some kids refuse to leave a place even if it's for their own good."

"I hope so, Uncle Bart. I don't think I could stand to see that." The image made my appetite disappear, and it took a lot to do that. "I can't figure her out. Somebody's gotta be looking for her."

"Unless they just dropped her off and drove away. I've seen worse."

Just hearing the words twisted my guts inside out. "I don't know how you live with what you see. I'd lose my mind."

Uncle Bart studied the table. "I've lost my composure a few times." He was seeing something in his head.

He snapped out of it. "After CPS gets here I'll drive you back to the house. You've had a full day and it's not even noon. You can rest and watch the Rose Bowl. I wanna follow up on some things."

"If it's all the same, I'd rather hang out with you."

Uncle Bart smiled. "I knew there was a cop somewhere in you."

I didn't correct him. Didn't seem the right time to do such a thing.

He carried on. "I've got Millie making calls to the other LEOs. Maybe someone in some other county knows something."

"Leos?"

"Law Enforcement Officers. Other cops in other departments."

"Oh. Thanks for letting me help, Uncle Bart."

"As I said, Tank, I'm thanking you."

We ate in silence for a few moments—even Littlefoot—then Uncle Bart said something that nearly knocked me off my chair.

"I know about what happened, Tank. I know about your football."

Back to the Tracks

3:02 p.m.

The rest of the morning and the first part of the afternoon passed slowly. I continued to worry about Littlefoot although she showed no signs of distress. She had eaten half of the cheeseburger and downed about a third of the milkshake, doing her dog-licking-peanut-butter-from-the-roof-of-its-mouth after each sip thing. On one hand it was funny, but on the other kinda sad. Nonetheless, she seemed to enjoy the meal.

Still, she never spoke and never moved from any chair I placed her in. She didn't show much reaction to events around her. I continued to study the paper she'd given me but I could get nothing out of it. It was gonna take someone a lot smarter than me to figure it out, and a part of me worried that even the smartest man or woman would walk away as confused as I was.

The paper fascinated me, but even more fascinating was the girl's response to it. When we first saw her, she stayed away from everyone but me, then, once we were in the station and asked for the paper, she handed it over. She showed no interest in it after that. None. One moment she seemed to guard it with her life; the next she no longer cared. It was as if I was meant to have the message and once she delivered it, she was done with it completely.

The problem was, I had no idea what I was looking at or why she would want me to have it. As is often the case in my life, I had more questions than answers.

I had something else on my mind: Uncle Bart's revelation that he knew about me and football. I didn't know what he meant, but I could guess. He didn't bring it up again. I had the feeling he was leaving that up to me.

At 2:30 or so Child Protective Services showed up. Two women—one looked fresh out of college, probably a sociology major. She looked to be about my age. Maybe a couple of years older. The other woman could have been the young social worker's mother. She was maybe fifty-six, round in the face and in the belly. She had the look of a grandmother and I thought that was perfect. It's easy to trust grandmothers. Grandmothers stood for milk and cookies, pies, hugs, tickles, and kisses on the top of heads. They say there is no love greater than that of a parent. Grandmothers may be the exception.

They came into the station, showed some identification first to Millie, then to Uncle Bart who came out of his office when he heard them arrive. Littlefoot showed no fear, and when the grandmotherly woman held out a hand, she slipped from her chair and took it. My heart shriveled in my big chest, a raisin alone in an empty warehouse.

I stood just outside the station's doorway and watched as Littlefoot crawled into the backseat of a county sedan. The grandmotherly woman joined her; the young woman slipped behind the steering wheel. I took a few steps closer and waved goodbye. Littlefoot bent forward and I could see her pure face.

She was staring back.

With green eyes.

The image was still playing in my mind when Uncle Bart pulled the patrol car to the side of the road, to the same place in front of Old Man Weldon's spread. During the drive he told me what he was up to. He wanted to follow the tracks again, this time in the opposite direction.

"Since we know the tyke is safe, we can take a little more time with our search. She had to start her hike from somewhere, I want to know where."

That made sense. "Couldn't the helicopter do this faster?"

He nodded. "It was needed elsewhere. Once we found the girl, the pilot had to move to some other pressing issue in the county. Besides, we can get a better feel for things walking the ground."

That made sense, too.

We exited the car and followed our own tracks from earlier to the spot where Weldon first led us. Snow had filled in things some, but not as much as I had feared. Oddly, the snow filled our tracks more than Littlefoot's. I'm not sure how that can be, but then none of this made much sense to me.

"Okay, son, let's see if we can't find out where this journey began. If we can find the where, then we might find the why. Police work often works that way. You'll learn that in time." At some point, I was going to have to break Uncle Bart's heart.

We started backtracking Littlefoot's journey. We encountered another fence and the tracks looked as if she had either walked straight through the split rails or levitated over it. Both ideas were impossible, yet that's what the tracks showed.

We continued on. Mostly in silence. I worried about Littlefoot and decided to distract myself with a different kind of unpleasantness.

"Uncle Bart, what did you mean when you said you knew about my football?"

He was slow to answer. He took a breath, then blew it out like a smoker emptying his lungs. "Straight up, Tank?"

"I think that's the best way to go."

"I know you were cut from the team."

And there it was. "Dad?"

"Yeah, he called about a week ago. Figured he should let me know since you were going to be up here. I gotta ask, Tank—is that why my brother didn't come up to watch the game this year?"

A wave of shame washed over me. "I hate to say it, Uncle Bart, but yes. He's—angry with me."

"Angry?"

"Furious, really."

Uncle Bart chuckled. "He's always had a short fuse. The stories I could tell."

"I haven't seen him since I moved from Southern California to Washington. He was proud as he could be of the football scholarship. I've let him down. Big time."

"Mind if I ask what happened?" He didn't look up from the tracks. "I'm not trying to butt in, son, just trying to be a good uncle. Was it the injury?"

"No, not really." How did I explain? I'd reviewed everything in my mind time and time again and it was all so weird that I barely believed it myself . . . and I lived it. "Players get injured all the time: concussions, broken bones, hyper-extensions; I guess there are as many possible injuries as there are body parts, so a busted toe is nothing new. I was third string anyway, being new to the university and all. I was still learning the plays the team uses."

"So if it wasn't your toe—how is it by the way?"

"Okay, it hurts, especially in the cold, but the doc says it's healing up pretty good. I should be back to normal in a couple of months."

"And here I've been dragging you through snow."

"No problem, Uncle Bart. It's just pain. I'm not making things worse."

We walked on another dozen steps, our gaze fixed to the tiny prints. "So, if not the toe, then what?"

This was the difficult part. "I needed to take a trip. Since I couldn't play, I asked if I could travel to Florida."

"Florida?"

I didn't look at him. It took all my focus to keep talking. "You know the friends I mentioned, the ones coming to Dicksonville." He said he did. "They needed me in Florida for something. Coach said I could go. What he didn't say was that real a football player wouldn't leave his team even if he couldn't play. He didn't say so, but I think he wanted me to prove my loyalty. Leaving told him I wasn't committed to the team."

Talking about it hurt, but I continued. "I should have realized that, but I'm not real good with subtlety. I blew it as far as the coach was concerned, and an injured, third-string guy isn't all that valuable."

"He should have been more upfront with you, Tank. He handled that wrong. All wrong."

"Maybe, but it wouldn't have changed anything. I would have gone anyway. I had to make a choice."

Uncle Bart stopped and stared at me. "Let me get this right, Tank. You had a full football scholarship to the University of Washington and blew it all off to go party with friends in Florida. That is the dumbest, most selfish—"

"It was no party, sir. No party at all. We weren't there to hang out."

"Then why were you there?"

I was getting frustrated. "Uncle Bart, you wouldn't understand."

"Try me."

I started walking again. "I've got a feeling you'll understand when this whole thing with Littlefoot is over. Strange things happen, and for some reason, me and my friends get pulled into it. I think it's a God thing."

"A God thing? You blame God for flushing your scholarship?"

"No, sir. I don't blame God for anything." This time I stopped and looked him in the eyes. "Weird things are happening. Don't ask because I don't have many answers, but let me ask you a question. When was the last time you tracked a little girl walking barefoot in the snow and who can pass through fences and levitate to the top of a barn? Have you seen anything like that before?"

"No, not exactly."

"Not exactly?"

He looked away. "Okay, never anything like that."

"We don't have answers, Uncle Bart, but somehow, some way we are all tied together in this and there isn't much we can do about it. I just know that it is the most important thing I've done or can ever do. I blew it on the football thing but I'd do it again if my friends needed me. I'd go to them, just like they're coming here—and I didn't call them. I was going to, but they were already on their way."

"How could they know?"

"Beats me. We'll find out when they get here."

We continued our hike in silence, then Uncle Bart said, "Just so you know, boy, I love you like my own son. You need to know that. I'm here if you need me."

My eyes grew wet. "Thanks, Uncle Bart. I love you too." A few moments later I asked, "Is that why you said I didn't need to go to college to get a job as a deputy sheriff?"

"Maybe."

We chuckled. The chuckles stopped ten steps later. We had found the end of Littlefoot's tracks, or rather the beginning of the tracks. The first steps were surrounded by a wide, circular depression in the snow. I figure it was thirty feet across.

Uncle Bart was the first to speak. "Maybe I was too quick to nix Deputy Wad's UFO idea."

I think Uncle Bart was right.

We both turned our eyes upward.

The IT

January 2, 3:33 a.m.

It was closing on Littlefoot. She ran. Screaming. Cold air pushed her hair back. Tears ran from her face. Her face. Her face. Dear God, her face. The fear. The shock. The panic.

I ran toward her. Through the snow. Pushing my bare feet through the snow to the frozen ground beneath. Shards of ice bit my feet, cutting them, jabbing them, shredding the skin. I couldn't stop. I wouldn't stop. I had to get to her first, before . . . before . . . the Thing did.

The Beast. The Animal. It was fuzzy, indistinct. I could hear its demonic yapping, like it was laughing. It found joy in Littlefoot's terror. I saw white teeth. I saw thick, black fur.

The IT was closing. Every stride moved it a couple of feet closer to its prey, to its evening meal, to my friend, to tiny, innocent, ten-year-old Littlefoot.

She screamed my name and dear God it burned my soul like acid.

Faster. I had to move faster. I could not allow It to catch her, shred her, dismember her . . .

Tears wet my face. The white field disappeared. The trees that lined the perimeter of the farm faded from existence. Only Littlefoot existed. Littlefoot and the Beast.

"Taaaaank!"

Her first word to me was born out of terror. Her first word a cry for help. A plea. A first word that could be her last.

I've never wanted to kill anything in my life, but I would rip the spine from the Creature, the It, the Beast, the Demon, the Spawn of Hell. I would make sure it never chased a child again.

My blood ran like lava through my veins; my heart was an airplane piston and my fury beyond description. My vision narrowed until I saw nothing but Littlefoot and the Predator. Something or someone was going to die tonight and it wasn't going to be Littlefoot.

I pumped my legs and for the first time wished I was smaller and faster. I needed speed now more than bulk.

Littlefoot fell. Face down. In the snow. She rolled to one side, glanced at the Sprinting Death, then turned to me.

She held out a hand and I was still too far away.

The Hound closed the distance. So did I. It leapt, its fierce gaze fixed on the little girl. It soared low, cruising toward the helpless child.

She screamed.

So did I.

It opened its jaws and snapped them shut.

On my hand.

I didn't care. The thought of her dying in this thing's mouth brought me more pain than I could process—I could feel nothing else. A powerful, violent bite was nothing in comparison. There were greater pains to worry about.

The Beast had my right hand in its jaws and was shaking his head as if trying to tear my hand from my arm. I found its throat with my left hand and squeezed. Harder. Harder until I felt its windpipe fold, until I felt my fingers press deep into its neck.

The IT bit harder. I couldn't feel the pain. I felt only fury, fury and fear for Littlefoot. Each second brought more anger, more hatred, more—

I screamed again and closed my left hand like a vice. Another scream—

I scrambled from my bed in Uncle Bart's guest room. Sweat covered my body, and my muscles were more tense than I'd ever felt them. A sheen of tears covered my face. My tendons strained to hold constricting muscles in place. I took in air by the bushelful, my fists were granite stones. My heart bounded in my chest like a caged ape trying to escape.

The dark room was lit by moonlight reflecting off the snow one floor below. I wondered if anyone heard me. Were my screams just in my head? I hoped so. I prayed so. I strained my ears to listen for footsteps, voices, or a knock on the door. Nothing. The animal part of my brain listened for the Beast.

"A dream. Thank God. Only a dream."

I was thankful. I didn't want anyone checking on me. I wanted to be alone—needed to be alone. I trembled like a captured mouse. I dropped to my knees, leaned over the bed, and wept.

It was an hour before I could pray.

At 5:15, I noticed the smell of coffee. There would be no more sleep that night and, truth be told, I wasn't sure I ever wanted to sleep again.

I dressed, hit the hall bath, then walked quietly down the stairs. A light from the kitchen splashed on a figure at the dining room. The figure's wide shoulders told me it was Uncle Bart. He sipped from a cup, set it down and stared at the table. He hadn't heard me. I didn't want to startle him so I cleared my throat.

"I heard you coming down the stairs, Tank. I ain't young anymore, but my hearing is as good as ever."

"Sorry, Uncle Bart. I hope I didn't wake you."

"Wake me? No I've been up for a little while. Can't sleep." He looked up. "What are you doing outta bed? I figured I'd have to drag you out around ten or so."

I faked a laugh. "I've never been good at sleeping in." I moved to the table. "I used to do extra work in the gym before classes."

"Get yourself a cup o' Joe, Tank. A man doesn't like to drink alone, even if it's coffee."

I did. I like coffee and this smelled better than any I had. I assume that's because it reminded me that all I had seen was just a dream. I found some dry creamer, doctored my coffee then moved back to the dim dining room. I preferred it dim for now.

Uncle Bart sighed like he was depressed or something.

I took a guess. "Bad dream?"

"Yeah, something like that." He took another sip. "You?"

"Yep. A doozy."

"Wanna talk about it?" He was trying to be a good uncle, but I could tell he didn't want to hear it.

"Nah. I'd rather forget the whole thing. You wanna talk about yours?"

He chortled. "Not in the least."

There was a catch in his voice and, dim as the light was, I could see his eyes were tinged with red. I assumed mine were too. "Littlefoot?"

"Yeah. You?"

"Yeah."

It was all we needed to say. We'd talk it about someday, but not now, not before the sun was up and we had been well lubricated with hot coffee.

We were on our third cup before we spoke again. It was a simple conversation.

"You hungry, Tank?"

I worked up a good smile. "I don't know what it's like not to be hungry."

After two three-egg omelets and more bacon than I should admit to, we both felt better. Auntie June helped herself to the leftovers, glad she didn't have to fix breakfast on a Monday morning.

Thirty minutes later I was showered, shaved, and dressed for the day. I almost felt human again, and the sharp edges of the dream had dulled some. I found Uncle Bart in uniform and strapping his Sam Browne service belt on. "Gotta hit the mean streets of Dicksonville, Tank. You wanna go or stay here and help June clean house?"

"Let me get my coat."

Where yesterday had been gray and stuffed with snow, today was bright and sunny. I imagined much of the white stuff would melt by the end of the day, except in the foothills where we saw Littlefoot's tracks. That snow would probably hang around for a couple of days, maybe a week. Still it was a good thing we retraced her steps yesterday. It gave us an opportunity to talk to some of the other ranchers, not that it did any good. They knew nothing of the girl and saw nothing.

Uncle Bart pulled onto Main Street, drove about a mile, slowed and began swearing. I followed his gaze. In the middle of the street, at about the same place as yesterday, stood Littlefoot, still barefoot, still in the same clothes. The sun was up, but the air was still cold.

"I don't believe this." Uncle Bart slapped the steering wheel. "I'm gonna have someone's head."

A car pulled around the little girl and slowed. I could see the driver's side window lower and a head poke out. Someone was checking on her. Uncle Bart turned on his emergency lights and the other driver saw it, waved, and slowly pulled away.

Uncle Bart had a little more rant left in him. "There's no way the girl could have walked back here. The CPS home is over thirty miles away."

"I'm not sure that's a problem for her."

"That's too weird, Tank. I know what we saw yesterday, but thirty miles? Really?"

"Weird is the new normal, Uncle Bart. Stop here. We don't want to scare her."

I glanced at him. Despite his outburst I could see that he was glad to see that she was safe. I know I was.

I exited the car and gave the girl a little wave and big smile.

No response. Just as before. I walked toward her. She looked up at me. Never had I seen a sweeter face. Her gaze was almost enough to erase what I saw in my dream. Well, almost.

I held out my arms and she reached for me. "Let's you and me go somewhere it's warm. I'll bet you're hungry. Do you like eggs?" Of course, there was no answer. Sometimes I can touch sick or injured people and they get well. I wish I could tell you it works all the time, but it doesn't. I don't know why. If it worked all the time, I'd spend my days walking through hospitals. Maybe that's why it doesn't. Maybe that's not my purpose. My hope was that my gift might work on Littlefoot and fix the reason she didn't talk. Maybe she didn't need fixing. I just didn't know.

It was only a two-block walk to the sheriff's station but in those two blocks I came to realize two things. First, I grew more depressed with each step. I don't get depressed too often and never for long, but I was feeling it today. There was a weight on my heart, like a car being dropped on a soda can. Maybe it was the dream. Maybe it was the shock of seeing Littlefoot back here, impossible as it was. I had no idea why I felt this way, but I started wishing the ground would open and swallow me. Take me away from all the misery in the world—

I shook off the idea. I had the little girl in my arms. That was my second concern. I didn't notice at first, probably because I was so glad to see her, but she was different. Littlefoot was smaller. She didn't *seem* smaller, she *was* smaller. I carried her yesterday. I spent hours with her. She was different today: tinier and lighter.

Impossible. But what about Littlefoot hasn't been impossible?

My feet grew heavier. My heart slowed. Strength poured from me as if there were an open faucet in my ankles. I was bleeding energy.

When I reached the sheriff's station, Uncle Bart held the door open. The girl buried her face in my neck as I heard a growl behind me . . . a familiar growl. I spun on my heel, ready to cover Littlefoot's body with my own. From the corner of my eye, I saw Uncle Bart reach for his weapon. He left it holstered and I saw nothing. No Predator. I shuffled in, made my way to one of the chairs where Littlefoot sat yesterday, and set her down.

"You okay, boy? You look spent."

I bent and rested my hands on my knees as if I had just finished a set of wind sprints. "I'm okay. Must be your cooking."

He took me by the arm and sat me near Littlefoot. "You rest there. If you're not better in five minutes, I'm calling the doctor."

"I'll be fine."

I saw Uncle Bart look at Littlefoot. "I'm gonna call CPS and find out who let a ten-year-old . . ." He stared at her for a moment. "Um, Tank—"

"I know. She's shrinkin'."

Reunion

9:03 a.m.

I was sitting in one of the holding cells in the back of the building. All of them were empty, they usually were, so I thought it might be a quieter, less frightening place for Littlefoot. Because she had changed since yesterday, I was tempted to call her "Littler-foot." Too hard to say and it might just confuse her. It was quiet back there. We were away from deputies and citizens coming and going.

The cell also had a bed and I was hoping my little friend would take a rest. She didn't look sleepy and I wondered, in light of all I had seen so far, if she even needed to sleep. I scolded myself. Of course she did. She had a body, right? She ate food, didn't she? Why wouldn't she need sleep?

I picked up the paper plates that had, moments earlier, held our breakfast. Yes, my second breakfast for the day. I wasn't the least bit hungry, but I feared that Littlefoot wouldn't eat unless I did the same. I introduced her to scrambled eggs, rye toast with jelly (she really liked that), and bacon. She avoided the plastic fork and used her hands to shovel the food from plate to mouth. To my surprise she ate everything and not once did she do the dog-peanut-butter thing with her tongue.

Uncle Bart had placed a call to social services to advise them that one of their charges was missing. He used colorful language and spoke loudly enough that the phone was probably unnecessary. That's when it occurred to me that things might be better back here in the cells.

"Tank." It was Uncle Bart. "You got visitors."

He stepped to the side, and the tall, gentlemanly figure of Dr. McKinney entered. "I knew you would come to no good, my boy." He said it with a smile. It took me a second to get the joke.

"Dr. McKinney!" I was on my feet and out of the cell. He raised both hands as if he could stop my approach. He wasn't much for hugs. I didn't care. I wrapped my arms around him and lifted him off the ground for a moment.

"Careful, Tank, he's old and frail." That voice sent electricity through me. Andi stood a step or two back from the professor. Her face was just a gorgeous as it had been a couple of months ago in Florida when I last saw her. Her red hair was still as bright and still defying gravity. I set the professor aside and gave Andi a big hug. I may have held the hug a little too long. She started to pull away. I don't know how to judge such things. I could see joy and humor in her eyes.

"Oh, sure, the white girl gets a hug."

I looked over Andi's big hair and saw Brenda's face. One corner of her mouth ticked up. It was the closest thing to a smile I had seen from her. Brenda was tough, streetwise, and at times, a little scary. She was quick with a cut and a great tattoo artist. I have some of her work on my arm, although I don't remember much about getting it. I took her in my arms. She hugged back. She could pretend to be as hard as nails but I knew about her softer side.

"I didn't expect to see you here, Miss Brenda," I said.

"Yeah, and don't think I'm not put out by that, Cowboy."

Something touched my leg. A small person stood by my right leg. "Daniel!" I scooped the kid up like a bundle of laundry. Daniel doesn't like to be touched, but he lets me get away with it. I set him down. "Secret handshake." I held out my hand and we went through a series of slaps and bumps. It takes about fifteen seconds, but the kid enjoys it. Me, too.

Uncle Bart cleared his throat. "You gonna play paddy-cake all morning or are you going to introduce me?"

"Oh, sorry, Uncle Bart. This is Brenda Barnick. She's a tattoo artist and a good one. This little guy is Daniel Patrovski. He's amazing in his own way. Brenda takes care of him some."

"Some?" Uncle Bart said.

"I'm his aunt."

Uncle Bart looked at her black face then at Daniel's white skin. "His mother know he's here?"

"He's got no mother. I'm the only adult in his life— well, me and this crew." She paused. "He lives in an institution most of the time but me and the professor, here, we been pullin' some social service strings gettin' him to stay with me more and more. We go on trips and stuff when we can."

I could tell Uncle Bart had a million questions, but he kept them to himself, his way of trusting me.

I took a step closer to Andi. "This is my good friend Andrea Goldstein."

"Pleased to meet you, Deputy." She held out her hand.

"It's Sheriff, thank you." At least he smiled when he said it. He took her hand, stared at her for a minute, then looked at me. I hate being transparent.

"Sorry." Andi looked amused.

"And Uncle Bart, this is Professor James McKinney. We just call him Professor."

"Ah." Uncle Bart held out his hand. "You the priest?"

"No, I'm the used-to-be priest. I travel the country and lecture now. Andi is my assistant."

Uncle Bart eyed the professor like he was checking him for a hidden gun. "What do you lecture on?" I cringed at the question.

"I help people get over the crippling belief in God and the supernatural."

My uncle's face hardened. "The crippling belief."

"Yes, sir. You see—"

I had to nip this in the bud. "How did you guys know I needed you? I was gonna call—"

"Which you didn't," Brenda snapped. "We ain't much of a team, Cowboy if we don't stay in contact."

"I know. Sorry. It's been a strange few months. I still wanna know how you knew to come."

Brenda, who was wearing an old, leather jacket two sizes too large, pulled a piece of paper from an inside pocket and handed it to me. I unfolded it. The paper was thick and I guessed she had taken it from an artist's pad. She had folded it three times, as if by doing so she could keep it safe and secret. Brenda was cautious. She didn't trust anyone and asked no one to trust her— present company excepted, of course.

I stared at the image. She had sketched it in pencil then traced it over in ink. I recognized myself. She had captured Littlefoot to a tee, and—

My knees went weak and my spine turned to Jell-O.

"Blessed Jesus."

I swayed for a moment. No one spoke, but I did hear Andi gasp. A hand grabbed my right arm. The professor. Another hand seized my left arm. Uncle Bart.

"You okay, son?" Uncle Bart sounded worried.

"He's scared." It was Brenda. "I ain't never seen him scared before. Ease up, Cowboy. You're with friends."

I was going to lose my breakfast. Both of them. I've trembled before, but only after I've over exerted my muscles during practice or a game. Never for any other reason. I couldn't stop quivering.

Something grabbed my leg. Correction. *Someone* grabbed my leg. It was Daniel and he held my leg as if he could hold me upright.

"Talk to me, boy." Uncle Bart spoke in a steady tone, a lawman's tone, but there were several gallons of fear hidden in his words.

I straightened, took several deep breaths, then handed the paper to Uncle Bart. He looked at it then said something that made me want to apologize to Andi and Brenda. Of course, I had heard Brenda use the term a few times myself.

"This was in your dream?" Uncle Bart's words were more than a question; they were a demand for information.

"Yeah. You?"

"Yeah."

"Again with the dreams," the professor said. "What's with this group and dreams?"

Uncle Bart snapped his gaze to the professor. "What's that supposed to mean?"

"It's hard to explain, Sheriff, and I don't believe in such things anyway."

"You don't believe in anything," Brenda snapped. "You've seen everything we have; you're just to stubborn too believe your own eyes and experiences."

"I'm not stubborn, I'm analytical."

Andi reached for the drawing. "What is that thing?"

I willed my heart to slow to a sprint before it unraveled in my chest. "The IT."

It took a full five minutes before I could stand on my own. "I'm okay now." I turned to Brenda. "When did you draw this?"

"The day before yesterday. Well, the night before yesterday. I was working late. I was inking a client's back. I drew that afterward."

I processed that for a moment. "You did this as a tattoo first?"

"That's how it works sometimes, Cowboy. You know that. I didn't even know I was doing it until I was done. I figured the client was gonna go ballistic since she came in for a Scottish castle. I lucked out. She was a Goth girl and loved what I did which is a good thing since tats are impossible to erase."

"Some girl out there has this tattooed on her back?" Uncle Bart asked.

"Yeah. Turns out, it's not the strangest skin art she has."

The professor crossed his arms. He wore a tweed coat with elbow patches. Real scholarly like. I hoped he had a heavier coat. What he was wearing looked good inside, but wouldn't do much outside after dark. "Tank, we've been traveling most of the day. Even with a flight to Medford, we still had a long drive out here. Maybe I could bother you to tell me why we're here."

I nodded. "Sure, professor. First, there's someone I want you to meet, then I need your permission to let Uncle Bart, I mean the sheriff, know about us. He's into this pretty deep, and he's family."

We didn't have any rules about secrecy, but we didn't much talk about our gifts and adventures. No one would believe them. I led them back to the cell where Littlefoot was waiting.

"Everybody, I want you to meet the greatest little girl in the world. This is Littlefoot."

"Littlefoot?" Brenda always came with a large stock of sarcasm. "Really? Littlefoot?"

"You'll understand when I explain things." I turned to the little one. "Little girl, these are my friends. They're here to help you."

Littlefoot slipped from the edge of the bed where she was sitting and walked forward. She looked at each one, then ten-year-old Daniel pressed through to the front and stepped in front of Littlefoot. They stared at each other for a moment: two silent children; two kids who didn't fit this world.

Then the miracle. Littlefoot smiled. I waited for angels to start singing. Daniel smiled, too.

Then Littlefoot's eye color turned silver.

"Um . . ." Andi began.

"Yes, we saw." The professor sounded stunned. Another miracle.

Chapter 6

It's All Greek to Me

11:15 a.m.

We sat in the break room. Uncle Bart had Millie put a sign on the door telling people not to disturb us. The privacy was appreciated. It took the better part of an hour to fill everyone in on all that it happened. None of my friends seemed stunned. The professor kept his detached skepticism alive, but it was part of his personality and I was used to it. At times he seemed like a swimmer being pounded by the waves but refused to believe there was any such thing as an ocean. We got along. I knew he thought I was a big, dumb jock, but there were days when he seemed less smart than me.

I told them about the tracks in the snow. Hearing that Littlefoot had been walking in the snow with no shoes made Brenda's hard crust crack. I saw her look away. Since I had been bawling like a baby in the wee hours of the morning, I wasn't inclined to judge.

I even told them of my dream—our dream—'cause Uncle Bart admitted to having had a similar nightmare. Except in his dream he failed to save Littlefoot. I didn't think my dream could be worse. Turns out I could have had Uncle Bart's.

It took some time to explain our group to my uncle. I told him about Andi's ability to see patterns in almost everything and make sense of things none of us could see; of Brenda's ability to see a bit of the future but only through her art; our belief that young Daniel saw things, people, angels, things that we couldn't. Of course, I admitted to my sometime-gift of healing.

"What about the prof, here?" Uncle Bart asked.

The professor lifted his chin. "I see reason where they see foolishness. I'm their ballast."

"Ha," Brenda said. "I see you more as a dead weight."

"And who was it, young lady, that paid for your airline ticket? You'd still be hitchhiking up Interstate 5. It's a long way from southern California."

Andi took over. "That's enough, Professor." Andi was the only one who could handle the man, although he never made it easy.

"Let me see if I got this right." Uncle Bart leaned back in his chair. His leather Sam Browne belt squeaked with the movement. "A crazy school in southern California with a well that reaches to the spiritual world; a house that haunts instead of being haunted; birds dying mid-flight and hitting the ground with their eyes missing—"

"And other animals too," Andi said.

"And that was in Florida." Uncle Bart scratched his chin. "Where Tank resurrected your dog." He went from scratching his chin to rubbing his eyes. "All I wanted to do was watch the Rose Bowl."

"I know it's hard to believe, Uncle Bart—"

"Hard to believe? That ain't the problem, son. I saw what turned out to be a little girl's footprints on the snowy roof of a two-story barn. You could tell me Martians landed just outside of town and I'd believe ya. I just gotta process it. That's all."

I looked at Littlefoot. Millie had run to the diner and picked up a couple of milk shakes for the kids. You know, to give them something to do while the big folks talked. Littlefoot took a sip, then did the peanut-butter-dog thing again with her tongue. Daniel took a sip and did the same. It was good to have something to smile about.

We batted around some of the weirdness involved with Littlefoot, then the professor made a request. "All of this is well and good, but you said you had a document you wanted me to examine."

Uncle Bart rose from his chair, then exited the room. The sound of a metal file drawer opening and closing rolled through the open door. My uncle reappeared with the small scroll. "He ya go, Professor. See what ya make of that. Lord knows I've got no idea."

The professor opened his mouth to speak, most likely to make a wisecrack about Uncle Bart's use of "Lord knows," but a sharp jab from Andi's elbow changed his mind. The others leaned in to take a look, too.

"Don't just sit there, Professor," Andi said. "Share your thoughts."

"He just handed the thing to me. I don't have any thoughts."

That made Brenda laugh.

Andi pressed her lips into a line. I expected something snide to come out of that mouth. Instead I heard, "We all love the way your mind works, Professor. Share your thinking."

Okay, maybe that was snide.

The professor cut his eyes her way, then turned them back to the document. He rubbed one of the corners like a man feeling the fabric of a fancy suit. "Doesn't feel like paper, at least the kind we're used to." He held it up to the overhead lights, then frowned. "Sheriff, I need a flashlight and a magnifying glass." He then added, "Please."

"I can do that." Uncle Bart disappeared from the room again and returned a couple of minutes later. "This do?" He set a heavy, metal-case police flashlight on the table. It was the kind that could be used as a baton as well as a light source. I knew I'd hate to be hit with one of those. He also set down a magnifying glass, the kind with a rectangular head and a small light.

"Yes." The professor first set the flashlight on its base. "Andi, hold this so it doesn't fall over. She did. He turned the light on and a spot of illumination appeared on the ceiling. The professor stood and set the paper on the business end of the light so the beam shown through it. Starting with the upper left corner, he moved the paper back and forth over the light, his eyes fixed on it, often bending close as if looking at a tiny bug.

"Interesting."

"What's interesting?" Brenda asked. Patience wasn't one of her virtues.

"Hang on . . . Hmm." The professor repeated his actions. "No watermark."

"What's a watermark?" I asked. I don't mind appearing ignorant so I ask a lot of questions.

"On some papers, especially fine papers, the manufacturer places its watermark. Sometimes you can identify the source of a paper. No help here. Of course, not every paper has such a mark. In fact, I'm not sure this is paper."

"Not paper?" Uncle Bart said. "It sure felt like paper to me."

"With all due respect, Sheriff, could you tell the difference between typical paper, vellum, and parchment?"

"Probably not."

"It isn't difficult, really, once you know the difference. Paper is made from plant material, vellum and parchment are made from animal skins."

"So that paper is made from an animal?" Uncle Bart said.

"I doubt it." The professor sat again and moved the flashlight to the side. He used the magnifying glass to study the document. "No fibers, no sign that it was once an animal." He leaned back. I don't know what to make of the material."

"And the writing?" Brenda shifted in her seat. She was getting antsy. When I first met her she was a smoker. She's been trying to quit but for people like Brenda, quitting was a long slog up a steep hill.

"That's another mystery." The professor leaned over the paper and put the magnifying glass to work again. "It's live ink—"

"What's live ink?" Brenda snapped. "You screwing with us, Professor?" Yep, she was antsy.

The professor didn't snap back. Not that he was a patient man. He wasn't. He wasn't a perfect man, either. When we were at Andi's grandparents' home in Florida, he admitted to being an alcoholic. I guess alcoholics believe they will always be an alcoholic. Anyway, he was one who no longer drank. I have yet to get the whole story on that. Perhaps he recognized his own symptoms in Brenda.

He continued to study the images. "It means it was written with ink by hand, not printed on a press or by a computer printer. A real hand wrote with real ink. Live ink."

"Does the ink tell you anything?" Uncle Bart asked.

The professor shook his head. "That's beyond my education and experience. To get real answers the ink and paper need to be analyzed by experts." He rubbed his chin. "The writing is a puzzle. At first I thought it was a form of ancient Hebrew. Not too old. Not paleo-Hebrew, something more recent, but I doubt my first assumption. It seems to be based on an early pictograph or logogram—um, characters that are based on pictures. Like Egyptian hieroglyphics. It's an interesting form of writing, but has many shortcomings. Most writing that began as pictures became more alphabetic over time. As language grows, so does the need for ways to communicate through writing. I suspect that's what we have here."

"Can you read it?" Andi asked.

"Oh, my no. I can't even identify it. I've never seen anything like it." He passed the paper to Andi. "Do your magic, Andi."

She pulled it close, studied it for a few moments. "I can't tell much. It has forty-two lines, each line has twenty-one characters. Twenty-one, that's half of forty-two. The space between the lines is even. I can't see any variation. It's almost machine-like which contradicts your idea that it's handwritten."

"Maybe," the professor said. "Keep going."

Andi was a wonder to watch. She saw what no one else could. I once saw her staring at a kitchen floor of fake-marble tile. In a few moments she determined that the tile had been manufactured with six different patterns. She also knew that the tile layer had followed a pattern that kept him from putting identical pieces next to each other. "I could marry a man like that," she had said.

That made me a little sad.

"The kerning—the space between letters—is just as uniform," she went on. "To be honest, I can't tell if I'm supposed to read this from left to right, right to left, or up and down." She kept her eyes on the document. "Okay, there are 882 characters or symbols or whatever they are. There are . . . fourteen different characters each repeating on an average of . . . never mind, that kind of average doesn't help. One character repeats 126 times— oh, that's three times forty-two—and one character that repeats only six times. Hmm. Six goes into forty-two seven times."

Uncle Bart looked at me. I shrugged.

"Forgive me for saying so," Uncle Bart said, "but I'm not sure what to make of all this."

The professor answered. "Well, neither do we. Not yet. I suppose it's like you investigating a crime scene. You don't start with the answers, you start with evidence. Some of that evidence will be useless, some of it will lead to a conviction. At the time you gather it, though, you have no idea what's valuable and what's not."

"Okay, I'll give you that."

Someone knocked on the door. It was firm yet somehow polite.

"Come." Uncle Bart said.

Millie poked her head in. "Social services will be here in about ten minutes, Sheriff."

"Thanks, Millie."

I caught Brenda looking at the children. I wonder how Daniel would respond when they took Littlefoot away.

"I want to try something." The professor pulled the paper away from Andi. "I need your help, Tank."

"Sure."

He picked up a pad of lined paper from a stack on the table. "Mind if I use this, Sheriff?"

"Help yourself."

He rose and rounded the table to where Littlefoot and Daniel sat on the floor, their milkshakes apparently gone. The professor sat on the floor in front of them and offered the first genuine smile I had ever seen him give anyone. "Come sit with me, Tank. I want our new friend to feel safe."

I did, lowering myself to the thin carpet that blanketed the floor.

The professor set the paper face down on the floor in front of Littlefoot. He turned it several times, then waited. He smiled at her. She didn't smile back. It seemed those smiles were reserved for Daniel. Littlefoot looked at the blank side of the paper, then at the Professor. He motioned for her to take it. He was relaxed and seemed to enjoy interacting with the girl. I had a feeling he had been a good priest.

We waited a few moments. I wasn't sure what the professor was up to, but I trusted him. The room grew quiet as a tomb.

Littlefoot looked at what had been her scroll, then picked it up and turned it around.

"Well, at least we know which edge is the top of the page."

That was clever. And simple too.

The professor patted his chest. "James." He did it again then wrote his name on the pad. He pointed to the word he had just written then at himself. Littlefoot watched as if she found the whole thing as interesting as a television show.

He pointed at me. "Tank." Then he wrote my name on the pad. "Tank."

She blinked a few times. Looked at the paper and then pointed to the first four letters on the first line. "Hel-sa."

Her first word. It sounded like music to me.

The professor laughed and clapped. Littlefoot—I mean Helsa—did the same. Even Daniel looked pleased. The professor held out his hand and she returned the paper. He then gently took her hand in his and gave it a little kiss. Another first. The girl giggled.

The professor rose and returned to his seat. I did the same.

"And what did that accomplish?" Brenda asked.

"Several things." The professor worked his smart phone. "First, we now know where the top of the document is, something we need to know if we are to decrypt it. We also have sounds we can attach to the first few letters. And . . ." he studied his phone, then raised an eyebrow. "We also know Littlefoot, as Tank likes to call her, is really Helsa. The name sounded familiar. It's Hebrew. Now, don't go crazy on this—" he looked at me when he said it—"but it sounded familiar because Hebrew has a similar name that means 'devoted to God.'"

Devoted to God. I liked that.

A Knife to the Soul

January 3, 6:30 a.m.

I was walking through the snow with no shoes on. Just like Littlefoot . . . Helsa. I was alone, trudging against the icy wind. If I came to a fence I would rise above it and gently settle on the other side. If I encountered a building—a farmhouse, barn, any structure—I simply floated over it. It made no sense to walk around when I could sail over with no exertion on my part.

My feet were cold. Colder than I had ever felt them. Even my nagging, almost-healed toe was numb. Still I moved on to a destination I didn't know for a reason I couldn't understand.

There was the sound of the wind and nothing more.

At first.

Then there was another sound. Dark, close, evil. I stopped to look around. Nothing but white fields and my footprints trailing behind me in a straight line. I turned my face to my destination, whatever that was. All I knew was I had to keep going forward.

The growl startled me.

The smell unsettled me.

The presence was similar to . . . to what? To my dream. Was *this* a dream?

Something touched my shoulder. I turned. Teeth. Black fur. Black eyes. Rancid breath.

Heart stopped.

Breathing seized . . .

"Hey, boy. Wake up."

The hand was still on my shoulder, but my surroundings had changed to something familiar. The snarling had turned into a human voice. Uncle Bart's.

"You okay, son? You were thrashing like nobody's business."

I took a deep breath. "Wow. Oh my aching soul." I sat up in the bed and swung my feet over the side of the mattress.

"Another nightmare?" Uncle Bart was already in his uniform.

"Yeah. I was about to have my face chomped off. I wasn't looking forward to that."

"Ya think?" He studied me a moment. "Good news is, you have the same ugly face."

"Hey!"

"Jus' razzing you, boy. Nothing like a little laugh to scare away the dark thoughts."

"Right. I appreciate it." I didn't have the heart to tell him it wasn't working. "I don't suppose you had the same dream."

"Nope. I woke up at four and decided to drink massive amounts of coffee. I didn't want to risk going back to sleep."

"You are a wise man, Uncle Bart." I stood and winced.

"What's wrong? Toe actin' up."

"No." I sat again and turned on the nightstand lamp. I hoisted up a leg and looked at my feet. They were red and a little tender."

"Let me see, son."

"I think I'm okay."

"I said, let me see."

There was no arguing with Uncle Bart.

"I could be wrong, but that looks like the beginning of frostbite."

"I haven't been outside." I thought of the dream. Couldn't be.

"Let me see your other foot."

I did as I was told.

"Looks about the same. Just red. No damage that I can see. You wanna see the doctor?"

I shook my head. "It doesn't hurt that much. Just caught me off guard."

His cellphone rang. "And so it begins." Uncle Bart answered and listened. "I'm on my way."

He turned and for a moment I thought someone had stabbed him in his heart. "That was Wad. It's Helsa. She's back in town."

I didn't want to believe what I heard. Social services had picked Helsa up yesterday afternoon. I watched them drive away with her. I don't forget pain like that. We spent the rest of the afternoon getting the team settled in one of the few hotels in Dickensonville, having dinner, and trying to figure out what was happening.

"I'll get dressed in a flash. I wanna go with you."

"Tank—"

"I'll be quick. I'll get breakfast later."

"Tank."

His somber tone frightened me more than the monster in my dream. "What? What's happened?"

"She's hurt. She's been . . . she's been stabbed. Wad called for an ambulance. We'll meet him and the girl at the hospital."

I wish I could tell you what I thought, the worries I had, the anger I felt, but my brain shut down. All I remember of the next few moments was praying, one of those very short prayers repeated over and over: "Dear Jesus, dear Jesus . . ."

Uncle Bart wasted no time getting to the hospital. County Hospital was an extension of a larger facility in Everett, near the coast. It was small by comparison, but it had great facilities and doctors. I think Uncle Bart told me that to comfort me. It's what people shared to make the worried worry less. "Oh, that's a great hospital. Your loved one is in good hands." I could appreciate that, although I admit I was in no mood to be comforted.

A little girl had been stabbed. Stabbed! Who stabs a little girl? Normally, I am balanced. My emotions seldom get out of control. Sure, I know worry. Sure, I know anger, but they have never taken over. I wasn't sure I could say that five minutes into the future.

The drive took ten minutes longer than eternity. Cars pulled to the side of the road as Uncle Bart, still mindful of the patches of snow and ice, stomped the gas, emergency lights flashing around us.

"You know we won't be able to do much when we get there, right?"

"I know, Uncle Bart. Maybe."

"Maybe . . . oh, your gift." He fell silent. "Shoot straight with your old Uncle Bart. Have you ever healed anyone? I know Andi says you resurrected her dog, but that's a tad hard to believe. You're not Jesus."

"It's true, Uncle Bart, and what you believe or don't believe makes no difference." My conscience gave me a sharp punch in the gut. "I'm sorry. That sounded harsher than I meant it to."

"I understand, son. I'm scared, too."

Tears made it hard for me to see. "I don't have many answers. I don't know why this gift only works sometimes. I tell myself that it has something to do with God's will, but I can't be sure." I looked out the side window and tried to focus on the passing terrain, illuminated by blasts of lights from the light bar. "I busted the leg of a lineman in a game. That was my first year at the junior college. Shook me up pretty good. I could see one of his leg bones trying to push out of his uniform pants. The guilt ate at me. I dropped to my knees and laid a hand on him. He was screaming. The pain was too much for the guy. I prayed and he stopped screaming. I was afraid he'd died or something, but when I opened my eyes, he was staring at the sky. I couldn't see any pain in his expression. The trainers arrived moments later and pushed me away. I took a couple steps back, looked at his leg again. The ragged lump where the bone had been trying to bust through was gone. Only a patch of blood remained."

I took a deep breath. "They cut away his uniform. I guess the blood told him his leg was busted, but the leg looked fine. He walked off the field."

"Tank . . . that's too amazing to believe."

"I know. I don't talk about it much. It confuses me. Still, have I ever lied to you?"

"No, but you did keep secret the fact that you had been cut."

"I've been feeling like a loser of late. I didn't want to relive the whole thing over."

"I guess I can understand that." He drove for another mile before speaking again. "When you said you wanted to carry Littlefoot the last couple o' blocks to the station—"

"Yep. I was hoping that God would heal her feet and whatever else might be bothering her. Turns out she didn't need healing . . . then."

A quick look at Uncle Bart told me he was thinking a big thought. "When this whole thing began and we were talking to Old Man Weldon—"

"Yes. I prayed for him."

"I wonder how he's doing."

Another mile passed.

"Tank, I'm gonna say something, and I want you to let me get through it before writing me off. This is gonna seem bad timing on my part, but I gotta say it."

"Okay."

"When we started this little adventure, I was trying to talk you into becoming a cop. I was trying to help you by giving you a goal after losing your spot on the team. I still think you should be a cop, but now I have a different reason." He cleared his throat as the next sentence got caught in his throat. "This is tough business and it's easy to lose perspective, to avoid getting close to those we help. You have the biggest heart I've ever seen. Cops everywhere could use a reminder of why we do this work. You have relationship skills that can't be taught. Let's say you do have the gift to heal—"

"Sometimes. I can't control it."

"Okay, you *sometimes* have the gift of healing, but your real gift is something greater. You see the good in everyone. I can only see the bad. You are a tonic, son. A real shot in the arm."

"I can't commit to anything now, Uncle Bart."

"I know that. I know it. I have one more thing to say. I don't know what to make of your friends, your team, whatever you consider yourself, but I think you got something waiting for you. Something to do. A mission. Yeah, that's it, a mission."

I didn't know what to say. I sensed he was right, but at that moment I couldn't think about life missions because Littlefoot was in trouble. Fear had me quaking on the inside. Portions of my brain were shutting down as if my mind wanted to keep things from escaping. Dear God, I was lost.

We rounded a corner and the hospital came into view. It was a two-story structure common in small towns. It looked new and modern and I did my best to convince myself it was a place of healing and not a great big crypt.

We pulled into a parking place near the emergency room and parked next to another patrol car. I assumed it belonged to Deputy Wad.

The next thing I remember was standing in the waiting room of the ER. Uncle Bart was next to me and Deputy Wad stood in front of us. His uniform was covered in blood.

"Deputy Waddle," I said. "You're hurt."

He looked at me, his eyes wet. Something about him was different. "It's not my blood, Tank."

I began to shake.

Hospital Rounds

1:10 p.m.

I thought time had passed slowly in the patrol car. Time in the hospital oozed by.

I'm no good at science or math, but I did have to take a couple of science classes in high school. One of my teachers told a story about Albert Einstein. Someone asked what he meant when he said time was relative: "Time spent with a pretty girl seems to go faster than time spent sitting on a hot stove." That's all I know about his theories, but at least that part made sense to me. We had been at the hospital over six hours, but it felt like we'd spent a decade in the waiting room. Relative time.

They wouldn't let me see Littlefoot. I thought about pushing the doctors and nurses aside. Not one of them was big enough to stop me and I was highly motivated.

But an invisible hand held me in place. At least that's how it felt to me. Reason came back. God could save her whether I was there or not. I'm not indispensable. I'm just one tool in God's tool kit. Not every tool is right for the job. So I did the tough work. I waited. And waited.

Deputy Waddle—I couldn't call him Wad after what he did for Littlefoot—filled us in on what he knew. He had been on graveyard shift. It was his week. He left the station to do another patrol before the day crew came in. He heard a scream. Looked down the street. Saw something a couple of blocks away, the same place we first saw Littlefoot, and something blurry. He rushed in her direction. He found her . . .

Sorry, it's a hard story to tell. I wasn't there but I could still see it.

Waddle found her lying in the snow, bleeding. He called for backup, found the worst wounds and tried to slow their flow—with his bare hands. Another deputy arrived to help and the ambulance came shortly after that. Then he called Uncle Bart from his cell phone.

To me, Waddle looked like a hero—a pale, blood-splattered, shaky hero.

"Seeing her lying in the middle of the street, in the dirty snow . . ." He swore. Shook. Then wobbled. I took him in my arms, bloody uniform and all, and held him. He cried, not like a child, but like a man who had seen brutality he would never forget.

We tried to get what information we could, but only learned that emergency surgery was needed and the doctors would talk to us later. I knew they weren't brushing us off, but it sure felt like it. Uncle Bart decided to go back to town and take Waddle with him. The deputy seemed too shaken to drive. "Give Tank the keys to the patrol car in case he needs them. You know, to get a bite to eat or somethin'."

I wasn't going anywhere.

Uncle Bart also wanted to check out the scene of the crime. Maybe there was something to be learned. Maybe.

The triage nurse in the ER directed me to a surgical lobby, a place where friends and family did the impossible work of waiting. I found a seat in the middle of a row of padded chairs, closed my eyes, and began to pray. It was the least I could do; it was the most important thing I could do. There weren't a lot of words, just a wounded soul crying out for help.

Several hours had passed when I heard the shuffling of feet. I couldn't, didn't want to open my eyes. Big as I am, some things are too heavy for me to lift, like swollen eyelids over red-rimmed eyes.

A gentle hand reached under my arm at the elbow. It was small. It was warm. It was tender. A moment later I felt the weight of someone's head on my shoulder. It was Andi. I recognized her scent, a scent I longed for many times. Uncle Bart must have told them where I was.

A larger hand rested on my left shoulder. A slight squeeze. A deep sigh. No words. Again, I realized that the professor must have been a good priest.

The acrid/sweet scent of cigarette smoke flavored the air. Normally I hate the odor, but this time it said Brenda was here. I heard her take a ragged breath.

Only one was missing: Daniel. But if Brenda was here, Daniel had to be here, too.

I opened my eyes and saw his small form in front of me, just out of arm's reach. I knew so little about Daniel. He saw things no one else did, he almost never spoke, but he had a courage no child should have to have. We stared at each other for a moment. I forced a smile. He burst into tears and ran into my arms.

He cried. I broke into sobs. Sobs loud enough to embarrass me. I was brought up to believe that men didn't cry in public, especially big guys like me. I wish that were true. It's not. I melted into the chair, comforted by the touch of four other misfits; friends as dear to me as family.

"They've been at it all night." Brenda moved to the seat the professor had vacated a couple of hours before. He and Andi had moved to the corner of the room, each fixated on their iPads. Brenda jerked her head in their direction. "They're obsessed with figuring out the kid's scroll."

"I'm glad they're working on it," I said. "I got no idea what it is."

"Me neither. I'm pretty useless in the intellect department."

"Don't say that, Miss Brenda. You're smart. Better, you're wise. We would be a much weaker team without you."

She studied me. "Is that what we are, Cowboy? A team? Really?"

"Yes."

"I dunno. We barely tolerate each other."

It was good to be talking again. "Teams fight, Miss Brenda. Don't let that throw you. My dad thinks football represents life. I think it's just a game, but he sees more. In some ways I think he's right." I shifted my bulk in the seat. "Look, I've been playing football since my Pee Wee days and it has taught me a few things."

"Like what?"

"I'm not a great player, but I get to play because of my size. I'm not the smartest guy on the field but I'm not dumb. We need the really smart, the really fast, the really strong, the really determined. There has to be a mix. That means players get on each other's nerves. They fight during practice; they fight in the locker room. They call each other names and blame one another for just about everything. Come game time, they are a unit. The other team is the enemy, not one another. So they pull together. Or as every coach I've had has said, 'Pull together or pull apart.' That's us. We bicker, but I know that when I need you—like right now—you'll be there for me. And I will always be there for you guys."

"I dunno, Cowboy."

"I do. Daniel needs you. Daniel and me are buds . . ." I turned to him. "Ain't that right, Daniel?" As usual, he didn't speak, but held up a clenched hand. I gave him a fist bump. "Daniel needs more than a buddy, he needs you. I don't know what part Daniel plays in all this but I know he's part of the team. I know you're part of the team. You are . . ."

"I'm what?"

"I was going to say that you are the perfect mother for Daniel."

She pulled back as if I had slapped her. She worked her mouth like she was going to say something but couldn't get the words to flow. She looked to me like someone with a secret.

She collected herself. "The way you said that makes me think you were going to say something else.

I hesitated.

"Go ahead, Cowboy. I'm tough. I can take it."

She had found a way to make me chuckle. "You're tough all right. Sometimes you're downright scary. I mean that as a compliment. What I was going to say is that there are days when I think you're mother to all of us."

"Shuddup! No way. I ain't that old coot's mother."

"He's not an old coot, Miss Brenda, the professor is just sixty."

"Ancient. A fossil."

"And you know how to handle him. It takes you and Andi both to keep on the path."

Daniel shot to his feet and looked to the far wall. I'm glad Brenda, me, Andi, and the professor were the only ones in the room. I didn't have to worry about what others would think.

"Daniel, what is it, honey?" Brenda slipped from her seat and knelt next to the boy. He continued to stare at the wall. "Is your friend-who's-not-Harvey back?"

He nodded. The professor and Andi stared at him.

Judging by the tilt of Daniel's head, his friend had to be seven foot tall. We're pretty sure he sees angels, so who knows how tall they are.

"Is something wrong?" Brenda asked. Daniel smiled, then the corners of his mouth turned down and his eyes widened. He turned sharply, stepped to me, took my hand and made me rise. I let him lead me to the waiting room door. He stopped.

Ten seconds later, a doctor appeared. "I'm looking for family of the young girl brought in this morning."

The others were on their feet a moment later. "She doesn't have family, Doctor. I'm Bjorn Christensen, her friend."

"That complicates things. There are laws that keep me from revealing patient information—"

Brenda stepped up. "Tank, Bjorn, is the sheriff's nephew. He's working with law enforcement on the little girl's situation." She sure knew how to take over a conversation.

The doctor studied Brenda the way a prisoner studied his executioner. "Still—"

"You want us to get Sheriff Christensen on the phone?" Brenda hit the last name hard.

"No. It's been a long morning."

He looked at the others, then directed his attention to me. "She came through the surgery, but she still has a long way to go. She lost a lot of blood and we had to keep hanging units of blood. We also did a lot of stitching, but she's gonna make it."

"Praise God," I said.

Brenda was still in control. "So the stab wounds were deep?"

"Those weren't knife wounds. Those are bite marks."

It was time for me to sit down again.

The professor found his seat. "I'm starting to hate this job."

Chapter 12

A Spark of an Idea

3:30 p.m.

Waiting is the toughest thing I've ever done. I have developed a high tolerance for pain. Hours in the gym and on the practice field have a way of toughening a man up. But waiting to see Littlefoot ate away at me. Of course, seeing her after the surgery, gazing at the bite marks might be worse, but I needed to be with her, to watch her little chest rising and falling, telling me she's breathing—telling me she's still alive. I needed that.

At least Andi and the professor had the scroll to occupy their minds. They stayed in their huddle looking at their iPads and whispering. They had taken digital photos of it and were examining every inch and every letter, or picture, or whatever it was on the document. My gaze lingered on Andi and I remembered how good it felt when she rested her head on my shoulder. I know it wasn't a romantic gesture. She was trying to comfort me. Still, it was a light in the darkness that swallowed me.

"Think they'll figure anything out?" Brenda walked back into the waiting room. After the doctor left, she had taken Daniel to find a bathroom and then for a walk through the halls. At first I figured she was trying to get his mind on other things. Although he seldom spoke, he seemed quieter now, if such a thing was possible. She may have been trying to get *her* mind on other things.

I shrugged. "If anyone can, they can. They're the smartest people I know."

"Thanks." Brenda tried to look hurt.

"You know what I mean."

"You know how to butter up a girl, don't you, Cowboy." She patted her dreadlocks as if trying to look prettier.

"I only meant—"

"I know what you meant, Cowboy. I'm just trying to pull you outta your funk. Not that you don't have a right to be in a funk."

I didn't know what to say to that.

She stared at Andi and the professor for a moment. "Hey, Computer Girl, I got a question for ya."

Andi looked up. "Computer Girl? Really? Computer Girl? Maybe I need a cape and some tights."

"You'd look good," Brenda said.

"Really?" Andi raised one eyebrow.

Brenda snorted. "No. I don't have the best schoolin' in the world but something occurred to me on my little walk."

"Like what?" Andi exchanged glances with the professor.

"What are the odds of us getting two messages in a row?"

"Two?" the professor asked. "There's another scroll?"

Brenda sighed dramatically. "Why is it that brilliant people are so forgetful?"

"Wait." Andi wasn't as forgetful as Brenda implied. "You mean that note you got when we were in Florida a few months ago?"

"Yep. The one the professor said to forget. The one he called a joke."

Andi furrowed her brow. "I looked at it and the page was blank."

"You peeked at it, girl. Tank saw the message."

I had seen it. In fact, I had read it out loud. We were getting ready to go to the airport. We had done all we could in Florida. A kid on a bike rode up and handed an envelope to Brenda. "That's right. I remember it."

"I don't," the professor said.

"That's because you declared it unimportant. A joke. You told us to forget it." Brenda pulled a familiar envelope from her coat pocket. It looked worn, probably because she'd stuffed it into various pockets over the past couple of months. "Wanna hear it again?"

"Stop being dramatic, Brenda. Just read the thing."

She cleared her throat as if she was about to launch into a speech. "Likewise you, human being—I have appointed you as watchman. Yechizk'el."

The professor's eyes darted back and forth like a Ping-Pong ball.

"Yechizk'el sounds familiar." I could almost see Andi's brain working.

"With your Jewish background, it should. Yechizk'el is the Hebrew way of pronouncing Ezekiel," the professor said.

"Like in the Bible?" I straightened in my chair. "Like the Old Testament prophet?"

The professor nodded. "Exactly, Tank. Exactly."

"So maybe we shouldn't have ignored it," Brenda said.

"Not necessarily, my young artist friend. As is, it doesn't mean much." The professor rose and moved to the seat next to Brenda. "May I?"

Brenda looked stunned. "Well, lookie who just found his manners." She handed it over.

Andi moved to sit next to the professor. "Odd handwriting. Squarish printing."

"Similar to the scroll, but using letters, not pictography." The professor rubbed his forehead so hard I thought he'd push his fingers through his skin. He shot to his feet. "Think James, think."

I don't think he was used to working this hard to make a connection.

"The phrasing is odd. It can't be from the original texts. *Human being*. That's not a term the Bible writer would use."

He paced the floor. I pulled my smart phone from my jeans, activated my Bible app and did a search for *human being*.

"Of course some newer translations might make use of the term."

"They did, Professor." I held up my smart phone. "There are several translations that use it." I looked at the phone again. "He does use the word 'human' several times."

The professor snapped his finger. "Son of man. If memory serves, Ezekiel used the phrase 'Son of Man.'"

"God uses it, Professor . . . I know, you don't believe in God." I did another search. Sure enough, "Son of Man" appeared several times. "Ezekiel 3:17: 'Son of man, I have appointed you a watchman to the house of Israel.' That's the first part of the verse."

"What translation?" The professor was staring at me.

"New American Standard. I have others."

"No, that's fine. It's a decent translation. A little too conservative in their renderings for my tastes, but respectable."

Brenda huffed. "I'm sure they'll be glad to hear you approve."

I expected Andi to defend the professor, but she didn't. Truth is, I've heard Brenda say worse to him.

"May I?" The professor held out his hand. I let him have my phone. He began to read:

"Son of man, I have appointed you a watchman to the house of Israel; whenever you hear a word from My mouth, warn them from Me. When I say to the wicked, 'You will surely die,' and you do not warn him or speak out to warn the wicked from his wicked way that he may live, that wicked man shall die in his iniquity, but his blood I will require at your hand. Yet if you have warned the wicked and he does not turn from his wickedness or from his wicked way, he shall die in his iniquity but you have delivered yourself. Again, when a righteous man turns away from his righteousness and commits iniquity, and I place an obstacle before him—"

The professor stopped suddenly and stared at the screen for a moment. He went pale. Before I could ask what was wrong he returned the phone to me and walked from the room without a word.

Andi looked at us. "What just happened?"

"I don't know." Brenda didn't offer a quip. She looked concerned.

"Tank?" Andi stared at me.

I lifted the phone and found the text that made him stop:

"Again, when a righteous man turns away from his righteousness and commits iniquity, and I place an obstacle before him he will die; since you have not warned him, he shall die in his sin, and his righteous deeds which he has done shall not be remembered . . ."

Brenda shuddered. "Yep, that would do it."

Andi stared at the door. "He sees himself as the righteous man who turned away."

"I think so," I said.

"He thinks God is going to kill him?" Brenda spoke softly so Daniel wouldn't hear, but my guess is he knew more than we did.

"Worse," Andi whispered. "The verse says the righteous man who commits iniquity will die and all his accomplishments will be forgotten. For an academic, that's worse than death.

Daniel stood abruptly. Looked at someone who wasn't there, at least as far as we could tell, then moved to the door and waited. A nurse appeared. She smiled, but her expression didn't seem genuine. "She's out of recovery and in a room now. You may visit, but please keep it short. She needs her rest. Room 227."

It took all my willpower not to run.

Chapter 13

Thirteen O'clock

5:30 p.m.

The sky was beginning to darken, but at these high latitudes, the sun set later than it did in Southern California. Light pressed through thin drapes illuminating tiny dust motes floating in the air. There was one bed, one IV unit, one chair, one television, and one lost little girl. I hadn't seen her when she reappeared in the middle of town early this morning. As before, as with each new appearance, she seemed younger, smaller, more needy. Looking at her, what was left of my heart shattered to pieces.

Littlefoot lay still as a corpse. Her body was covered in a white sheet that looked too much like a shroud. What was wrong with hospitals? A pink sheet, or a blue one, or just about any other color would be better than the lily white material that implied death. Maybe that doesn't make sense. My brain was on fire when I thought it.

I took two steps into the room. I heard Andi gasp behind me. Brenda whispered, "Oh God." It was the closest I had ever heard her come to praying.

Littlefoot—she would always be Littlefoot to me—didn't move when we entered. We tried to be as quiet as we could. Her face was lovely, her arms were a mess o' red, angry-looking bite marks. The sight of them brought images of her little frame in the jaws of a monster. I could imagine it thrashing her around as if she were a rag doll. Tears crept down my cheeks and I didn't care. Brenda held my right arm; Andi my left. I needed their strength. I needed their touch to remind me that there was still good in the world.

My mind was unraveling.

Daniel pushed by and walked to the side of the bed. I started to tell him to stay back, but it didn't seem right. Had it been any other kid I would have said something, but Daniel was, well, Daniel. He looked at her arms, something no kid should see. He looked at her face as if studying it for signs of life. Again he moved his gaze to her left arm and traced it with his eyes until he settled on a finger that appeared unharmed.

He touched it. The gesture was so light it wouldn't have moved a feather. I love that kid.

Littlefoot opened her eyes, eyes the color of unsweetened chocolate, and looked at Daniel. He smiled. She smiled. I had a feeling an entire conversation was carried on in those seconds.

Then she stuck her tongue out. In and out. It was the peanut-butter-in-the-dog's-mouth-thing again. Seeing that made me feel like things might be all right.

Daniel turned to Brenda. He didn't speak, but Brenda got the message. "I'm on it, honey." To me she said, "I'll see if the cafeteria has milkshakes."

I managed to nod.

"Tank?"

I didn't need to turn to know Uncle Bart had shown up.

"The nurses told me you guys were up here." He stepped to the spot Brenda had occupied. "How's she doing?"

"I just got here."

"She looks younger—again."

I nodded and walked to the right side of the bed. I moved under compulsion. Nothing in the universe could have kept me away. She turned her face to me and I stroked her cheek. Precious. Beautiful. Everything good in the world contained in one little girl's body.

Like Daniel, I studied her arms and hand. Her arms were swollen like sausages, the skin tugging against the stitches. The sight of them pulled my strength through a paper shredder. Her right hand had a severe bite mark, but her thumb was untouched. Using two fingers, I held her thumb and stroked her hair with my other hand.

A few deep breaths later I gazed into her eyes . . . that were now blue.

I closed my eyes.

The sounds were the first thing to go, then the room, the sense that others were present. All of that was replaced by darkness. It sounds strange to some, but God is often found in the darkness—in the holy dark.

It was warm. It felt safe. I had been here before, good had come out of—

The growl startled me. The scream brought me back. Littlefoot was sitting up in bed, her eyes white as chalk and looking toward the door. I snapped my head around. Andi was seated on the floor doing her best to back away from the doorway. Brenda was slumped next to one of the walls, a milkshake toppled and gushing its contents on the floor. Uncle Bart was struggling to get to his feet. He fumbled for his gun.

It was there. The black thing. The blurry thing I had seen in my dream. The thing with the white fangs— fangs that pierced the skin and muscles of Littlefoot. It looked at me with eyes that blazed like molten steel, then fixed its stare on Littlefoot. It took a slow step, then another. The remembered pain of my dreams was now alive.

Then it sprang.

So did I.

I don't know who made the most noise, the beast or me. We both screamed as we met near the foot of the bed. Its front paws passed over the foot of the mattress before I reached it with my right hand. I caught it at the neck and clamped my big mitt shut. It turned on me. Just like I wanted it to do. One claw ripped my right arm, the other caught my left shoulder. I didn't much care.

I pulled it close.

I embraced it, pulling it tight to my chest. If need be, we were going to die together, me and this attacker of little girls. Maybe I was born for this one moment; maybe not, but I did know that only God Himself could break my grip.

We hit the floor, me on my back, the It on top of me. It writhed. It twisted. It lurched. It snapped its jaws. Its breath reeked of rotted meat, a breath it inflicted on Littlefoot. That thought gave me new strength, new power, new purpose.

"Tank." Uncle Bart came into my vision but I couldn't pay him any attention. He had his gun drawn. "Tank, let go. I can't get off a shot with you holding it."

I don't know if shooting would have done any good. Besides, to let go was to let it rip out my throat. Instead, I tried to tighten my grip, but it pulled its head away.

The bite was crushing. I felt its teeth make contact with the bones of my arm. Fine. Instead of trying to pull my arm out, I pushed it farther into the beast's mouth. If it was going to eat me, then it was going to choke on me.

Uncle Bart moved closer.

"No. Stay back. Stay back."

I caught sight of Littlefoot. The look of fear on her face hurt more than the thing chewing my arm—

The hospital room vanished. The ceiling became a beautiful green sky. The ground was firm, but somehow different. The light was wrong, but I didn't know how. And I didn't have time to think about it. One thing I did notice was the fuzzy, indistinct, hard to see It had become clearer. I liked it better the other way.

A flash of light. A sense of falling and then I was flying through the air and back in Littlefoot's room. We hit the wall with the window. I heard the glass rattle—

The hospital disappeared again.

Then I was back.

I wrapped my legs around the Creature and continued to hold on. One of us would run out of energy sometime. I just had to make sure it wasn't me.

"Ta—"

Back in the green sky world, but this time I wasn't alone. Two people. Two men—I guess they were men. They were taller than me and wider at the shoulders and they looked very unhappy. I could only hope they were on my side.

The It clamped down. This time I was certain the thing would bite my arm off. I'd be dead soon after. I fought on. What choice did I have?

One of the men spoke and the It released its jaws and snapped its head around. Its eyes widened. I felt it tremble. With impossible speed, one of the men ripped the Beast from my arms with one hand. He lifted it high. Said something I didn't understand and then disappeared.

I glanced around, but can't describe what I saw. Things didn't make sense to me. The best I could tell, I was flat on my back on some open plain. There was grass beneath me. The horizon seemed to curve up instead of down.

The second man moved closer. He looked sad.

He smiled. It was a weird smile, like someone who wasn't quite sure how to do it. "Hi, Tank."

"You're . . . you're Daniel's friend, aren't you?" He nodded. I rolled to my other side, holding my bleeding arm. The thing had pierced an artery. If I let go, I would be dead in short order.

I looked over at my little friend. "Daniel?"

"Yep."

"What are you doing here?"

"I've been here before." He seemed to be a little older.

"Is this heaven?" I had had a glimpse of heaven in the House some months back, but it didn't look like this.

He shook his head. "Nope. It's a different place."

"Littlefoot?"

"She's good. This is her world." He crouched near me. "Time to go home."

I was on the floor. On my back. Clutching my wounded arm. Blood gushed.

"Dear God, Tank." Uncle Bart was at my side applying pressure to the wound. "We need a doctor. Now. NOW. We need a doctor, now."

I looked at Littlefoot. She looked well. Whole. Healed. Whaddya know? It worked this time.

Outside the window, the sun continued to provide light for the world.

Sunset pulled a thick blanket of black over me.

10:00 p.m.

"Man, my arm hurts."

I was in a hospital bed, an IV needle in my arm. It hurt. My other arm, where they did surgery, hurt; my back hurt, my head hurt. Oddly, my busted toe felt pretty good.

My friends were around me. So was the doctor who did surgery on Littlefoot.

"You've had a long day, Doc."

He laughed. "*I've* had a long day? You know, I used to work in a big city hospital. Saw it all there. At least I thought I did. I'm confused by all this. I don't even know what questions to ask."

"We don't either, Doc." Andi stood close to the right side of the bed. She looked like she had been down a long, hard road, but she looked good to me. Brenda was biting her nails. Even tough chicks get shook from time to time. The professor looked like a scolded dog and stood near the wall. He hadn't been in the room, but my guess is they told him all about it.

To make things better, I had another visitor: Littlefoot. She looked about six years old, and her skin was unmarked. Seeing that made me the wealthiest man in the world. She held a milkshake in one hand. Daniel had one too. Each time they took a sip, they did the tongue thing, then giggled.

"Give him the rundown, Doc." Uncle Bart managed to look worried and joyful at the same time.

"Okay. As you know, we did surgery on your right forearm. We had to repair a damaged artery and pick out bone fragments. You had several puncture wounds to your legs and torso, we assume from the creature's claws. You also separated a couple of ribs. You have a ton a bruises."

"'Ton of bruises,' is that a medical term?" Andi said.

"Don't mind her, Doc. She's a little too attached to details." For Brenda, it was a kind comment.

The doctor excused himself and said he was going home. He was done with the day. So was I.

We spent the next few minutes relating what we had seen. I told what I saw and even mentioned Daniel's appearance on the other side. "He looked older and he said it wasn't heaven. It didn't look at all like the heaven I saw in the House."

"I doubt it was heaven," the professor said.

"Oh, don't start, Professor," Brenda said. "We all know you don't believe in anything but your gigantic intellect."

That seemed to wound him. He looked more vulnerable than usual. "Let me explain. We think Daniel sees angelic beings. Now it appears that Tank does, too. According to Tank, one admitted to being Daniel's friend. And, of course, I had an encounter with something at the house. Maybe it was illusionary, I don't know. Anyway, I don't think Littlefoot is an angel. Not in the sense that we use the term today. Technically, the word *angel* means *messenger*, so anyone carrying a message is an angel. It that way, Littlefoot *is* an angel, but not an angelic being. Am I making sense?"

"I'm with you, Professor," I said. "For a change."

"This is hard to explain in a few words." The professor inhaled as if he hadn't taken a breath for an hour or so. "The world of science has turned things upside down of late. Quantum theory describes quantum entanglement, indicating that things in the subatomic world are somehow connected, at least in certain conditions. That deals with the very small things. On the cosmic level, many physicists believe that we live in a multiverse instead of a universe."

"Meaning what?" Uncle Bart asked.

"The idea is that all we see is our universe, but ours is just one of many others. They're similar but not identical to ours, and a new one is created each time we make a decision. And with so many decisions being made, these other universes can vary wildly. I know. I know. It's difficult to fathom, but there are many excellent scientists who have hung their hats on the idea.

"Each universe is independent of the others, but there might be ways to cross over. Then there's the whole multi-dimension thing that is totally different. Lots of folks believe there are eleven or twelve dimensions. But that's different because dimension deals mostly with spatial things. Most Christian thinkers, especially among conservative Protestants, believe that angels are beings from another dimension and can move between dimensions as is shown in the Bible. The truth is, there's a lot we don't know."

I looked at him. "My head is beginning to hurt."

He moved closer to the bed. "Don't worry, Tank. I don't expect you to understand. My guess, and that's all it is at this point, is that Littlefoot is from another universe close to ours and somehow related to it. Time flows differently for her. That's why she grows younger when she comes to us and why Daniel appeared older wherever you were. I assume you were in Littlefoot's land."

"You're breaking my brain," Brenda said.

I expected a cutting reply, but the professor let it pass. "I want to show you something." He extracted his smartphone and took a photo of me, then showed me the picture. I saw a few bruises, but the most shocking thing was the hair on my face. I rubbed my chin with my good hand.

"How long does it take for your beard to grow that long?" The professor kept his eyes on me as I handed his phone back.

"A week-and-a-half, maybe."

"I missed the action but they tell me the fight only lasted a few seconds."

"It felt a lot longer than that."

"When Littlefoot is here, she grows younger. When you were there you grew older."

"How can that be?" Uncle Bart wasn't used to hearing such things.

"I don't know, Sheriff. No one does. We are experiencing things that no one else has and we don't have enough information yet to give solid answers. Yet."

"Yet?" Brenda lowered her head. "You sayin' there will be more of this?" She added a term I'm uncomfortable with.

"Yes. Maybe the weirder stuff is yet to come."

Andi touched my hand. Just a finger or two. "You should tell them the rest," she said to the professor.

"It's about the scroll."

"You figured it out?" I hoped so. I don't like puzzles.

"Not completely. It might be impossible to understand fully, especially if it's a language from Littlefoot's universe. However, I think Brenda was right when she began to wonder if the message that was handed to her at Andi's was related. Some good thinking there."

Brenda snorted. "You make me blush."

The professor ignored her. "Andi and I spent the time you were in surgery arguing over this and reviewing the document. The first note was in English, but it looked as if a non-English speaking writer penned it. You already know—well, the Sheriff doesn't know since he wasn't there—but the first note was a variation of a passage in Ezekiel. Ezekiel experienced some very odd things: multi-faced beings, winged angels, God's throne on a set of wheels within wheels. We still don't understand all that he saw. If he really saw them." He raised a hand. "I know, I know, we've seen equally strange things."

"What's the point, Professor?" Brenda asked.

"I suspect that the verse given you was changed to fit our situation. Ezekiel was being set apart to be a watchman over Israel, and to call his people back to faith. Maybe we're being called to do the same thing. Not to Israel, but to the world."

"This is a calling, Professor?" I asked.

He looked like he was choking on a bone. "I think so. Tank, you've called us a team several times. I've always looked at our past adventures as a few bizarre happenings with no purpose, no message, no meaning. I'm not so sure now. We may be stuck with each other."

"So what's the mission?" I asked.

He shrugged. "I really don't know. Andi has noticed a few things in common."

"I need to give it deep thought, but we do know that in each case we've encountered opposition and things beyond this world and it has taken our combined skills to solve the problem, even to save lives. I think we've just started our journey." Andi sounded a little like the professor.

"Will you be able to read the whole scroll?" Uncle Bart asked.

"I can't. I've taken it as far as I can. I've sent digital photos to Cardinal Hartmann in the Vatican. If I may, I would like to send him the original document. I know he's going to ask for it. He's a genius with languages and I'm hoping his contacts in the Vatican might help. Brenda's message is from Ezekiel chapter three. It's not a modification of a verse as I first suspected. I found the exact translation in a Messianic Bible. At least we can understand that message. I can't be certain, but the two documents seem to be related."

"Not knowing is as much a part of being human as knowing, Professor," I said.

"Perhaps, Tank. Perhaps."

Littlefoot set her milkshake down, walked to the bed, touched my hand and smiled. Then she began to blur. At first I thought the drugs were affecting my vision, then I realized the creature looked that way when it came to our world.

"No. No stay, Littlefoot. I don't want to lose you." I tried to get up. The professor pushed me back in the bed.

"Let her go, son. She can't stay here. She will just get younger and younger, then what? She needs to be in her home just like you need to be in yours."

"But—"

"She has to go, Tank."

Littlefoot waved at me, giggled at Daniel, then waved at the others.

She was gone, and with her my joy.

Uncle Bart took me to his home the next day. He was holding a January barbecue for the others who were leaving later that evening. The snow around Uncle Bart's house was all but gone but the air was still cold so most of us stayed in the house. Mr. Weldon, the diabetic rancher, had been invited. He stood outside by the barbecue while Uncle Bart kept a practiced eye on the grill. I watched through a window. I was a little too sore to be outside shivering. Weldon looked strong, spry, and healthy. He looked at me and raised a cup of whatever he was drinking in an unspoken toast.

I guess sometimes I do some good.

FROM HARBINGERS 5
THE REVEALING

BILL MYERS

"What're you sketchin' now?" Cowboy asked.

I flipped my notebook shut like some kid caught with porn.

The big guy smirked. "You know, Miss Brenda, you don't have to keep hidin' your gift under a bushel."

I gave him a look. He gave me one of his good ol' boy shrugs. Daniel's sittin' on my other side and stifles a giggle.

I shoot him a look. "You think that's funny?"

He grins and imitates Cowboy's shrug.

I scowl. But the truth is I like that grin. It don't happen much, but whenever it does, it warms somethin' up inside me.

The sketch is a blue velvet armchair. It's got peeling gold paint on its arms. I've been seeing it ever since we got on the plane to Rome. Never left my head. Not during the eight hour flight with its crap food and rerun movies, not during Mr. Toad's wild taxi ride from Di Vinci airport to the Vatican, and not as we sat on this butt-numbing wood bench listening to the professor lay into some pimply-faced, man-boy receptionist.

"Well look again." The old man waved at the computer screen. "Cardinal Hartmann. You do know what a Cardinal is, do you not? *Cardinal* Hartmann invited us to this location at this particular date and this particular time to—"

"*Mi scusi,* Signor, but you cannot have an appointment with—"

"Blast it all, don't tell me what I can and cannot have."

"But, such a thing, it is not—"

"I'm sorry, are you part of some special needs program?"

"Professor . . ." As usual, Andi, his ever-cheerful assistant, stepped in to try and prove her boss was a human being. As usual, the odds were not in her favor.

Meanwhile, Daniel scooted off the bench to get another drink of water. At least that's what I figured. But the way he cocked his head upwards like he was listening, told me one of his 'friends' was around.

Miss Congeniality continued smoothing things over. "What the professor means is, we've just come from the airport. In fact we haven't even gone to our hotel because Cardinal Hartmann sent a very urgent and very personal request for us to visit him today."

Cowboy and I traded looks. It was true. It hadn't even been a month since the professor sent the Cardinal that scroll with the fancy writing on it. The one some kid, supposedly from another universe, gave us. I know, I know, long story and I'm not in the mood. The point is, this Cardinal guy, who used to be the professor's mentor back when the professor believed in God, begged us to come. He sweetened the deal by e-mailing each of us plane tickets. And since I couldn't cash them in, and the professor had pulled some strings to get us some quick passports . . . well, here we were with our ol' pals—stuck in some back-room reception area that smelled like old floor wax and old men.

I glanced over to Daniel. He'd passed the water fountain and stood at a wooden door built into the wall. Hardly visible. He looked back at me like he wanted something.

"*What?*" I mouthed.

He just stood there.

"*What?*"

Meanwhile, the professor cranked up his personality to Super-Jerk. "Okay, you do that."

The receptionist got up and headed out of the room.

"Only make sure you bring back someone with a rudimentary understanding of communication skills."

Daniel cleared his throat, real loud to get everyone's attention. We turned to him and he reached for the door. He pushed it open and motioned for us to join him.

"What is it now?" the professor said. "Do you wish for us to follow? Do you believe there is something inside there?"

Daniel sighed like it was obvious. And for him it probably was. Cause, like it or not, the kid heard things we never heard. Saw things we never saw. And whether the professor believed in any type of "higher power" or not made no difference. Our last couple road trips made it clear Daniel was connected to something.

So, without another word, Dr. Stuffy-Butt headed over to join the boy. Something was up and he knew it.

So did Cowboy. "What's goin' on little fella?" the big jock asked as he rose to his feet.

Daniel pointed to the open doorway. It was dark but you could make out some real narrow steps. Me and Andi glanced at each other then got up and followed. None of us knew what was going on in that little head of his, but, whatever it was, it wouldn't hurt to pay attention.

ABOUT ALTON L. GANSKY

Alton L. Gansky (Al) is the author of 24 novels and nine nonfiction works, as well as principal writer of nine novels and two nonfiction books. He has been a Christy Award finalist (*A Ship Possessed*) and an Angel Award winner (*Terminal Justice*) and recently received the ACFW award for best suspense/thriller for his work on *Fallen Angel*. He holds a BA and MA in biblical studies and was granted a Litt.D. He lives in central California with his wife.

www.altongansky.com

Catch up on all the Harbingers episodes!

CPSIA information can be obtained at www.ICGtesting.com
Printed in the USA
LVOW10s2350270716

498073LV00012B/157/P